L. JOHNSTON LEWIS

Cousin Birdlegs

CAN GULLIBILITY
REALLY BE OUTGROWN ?

AuthorHouse™

1663 Liberty Drive, Suite 200

Bloomington, IN 47403

www.authorhouse.com

Phone:1.800.839.8640

First Published by AuthorHouse 8/29/08

ISBN: 978-1-4343-1147-4(e)

ISBN: 978-1-4343-1146-7(sc)

Library of Congress Control Number: 2007903819

Printed in the United States of America

Bloomington, Indiana

This book is printed on acid-free paper.

DEDICATION

TO MOTHER & DAD

Whose Love showed the way; Who now look down from a Higher Plane and are probably still shaking their heads...

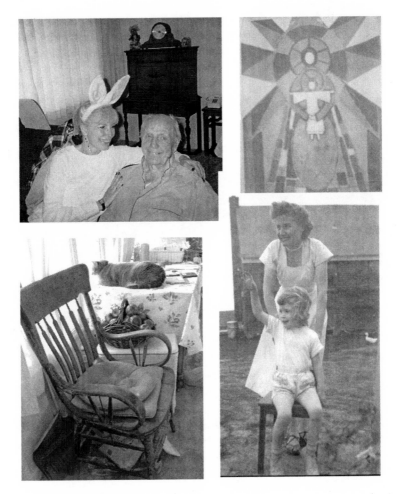

In the beginning...

These stories are firstly for those:

Whose earliest memories are of brand-new 9" black-and-white televisions, Ike & Mamie in the White House

In whose world every social nicety was explained in excruciating detail and usually involved the wearing of white gloves

Who were naïve, and innocent, and who had no concept of a world where really bad things lived

Whose worst fear was not living up to academic expectations grownups had prayed and paid for

Who believed in a nice traditional God who looked a lot like Charlton Heston or maybe Mr. Hemphill across the street

Who believed that doctors and lawyers and the IRS *always* had your best interests at heart and would never knowingly do you in.

Who were required to go along with parental justifications for cleanliness involving the absence of ripe gym socks under the bed and nasty apple cores with clouds of fruit flies.

Woven from divine days of innocence, these stories rekindle distant memories of mountains beckoning in moon-glow splendor, pollywog-to-frog miracles, peanut-butter-fingered piano recitals, and luminous summer skies awash in clouds of dragon's breath.

Here are laughter-filled escapades, primo summer gotcha's, tales of prank survival and adventures of boredom-driven Summer Cousins whose cosmic job it was to reveal with scientific clarity just how gullible an otherwise intelligent child could be. From the land of family legend, we bring you our bowlegged, naively goofy, exceptionally gullible, dear

Cousin Birdlegs!

ACKNOWLEDGEMENT

It was surprisingly difficult to disguise names of those who will recognize themselves throughout "Cousin Birdlegs." Even in large Iowa families there is a short list of traditionally acceptable names to go around, names which -- being stoically Midwestern -- generally do not include adjectives relative to one's perceived social shortcomings or hyphens ala Buford-Billy-Bob-Boudreaux.

In case some are getting antsy at the possibility of full disclosure in these tales, be it known that certain characters and situations have been politely blessed (and in one case heavily larded) with literary license and selective memory. If you think I'm talking about *you*, it's pure coincidence. This is fiction. That's my story and I'm sticking to it for the moment.

Grateful thanks to kinfolk who made sweltering summer vacations such an adventure for the terminally gullible. Please note there is no mention of the August *someone* avowed there was positively no indoor plumbing at Grandma's which resulted in midnight lantern-lit forays through spooky gardens to an abandoned spidery outhouse. Neither shall we name *someone* who opined that "eatin' the pollywogs will getcha a leg up on the rest of the family who hafta wait for oh *weeks* for fully-growed frog legs." And yes, they wiggled all the way down. And back.

Along the journey from black and white TV's to AARP-hood were those kind enough to suggest that gullibility could occasionally be outgrown. Three grandchildren have arrived and I'm still waiting but thanks anyway for the thought.

That skinny young girl is grown now and
The black-and-white's gone silvery-grey,
But the Magic remains, you can touch it
For it's Love, and Love knows the way.

Table of Contents

CHAPTER ONE

In the beginning was The Word...

It all began in earnest about the time Cousins Preston and Eldridge hit the G's in the old Oxford dictionary. Right near "gulosity" (with which Uncle George claimed they were afflicted) and just before "gully-hole" loomed "gullible."

"Easy, trustful, naïve," muttered thirteen-year-old Preston.

"Sounds better'n being a glutton which is what Oxford says 'gulosity' means. Hey, *you* were supposed to look this up! You're the one with the 'deplooorable vocabulary'!"

"'*Glutton*?'" winced his pudgy sibling. "Guess that means no more thirds on meatloaf, huh?" Brother Eldridge was deeply focused on yet another English essay due dour Mrs. Willa-Rae Weeblefonger first thing Wednesday which meant head-down stress-eating was on the menu for sure.

Preston Gertner whirled around from his battle-scared maple desk, scattering a homework blizzard. He just stared at his elder brother, jaw gaping like whales at a krill feast. Chicken-skin bumps galloped down his arms.

"That's *gross*, Eldridge! Anybody dumb enough to eat 'thirds' of that stuff should wear a warning sign: 'Beware! Meatloaf Freak. I eat Mom's mystery meat – and I *like* it!'" He then stuck an index finger into his mouth and made a most ungentlemanly noise.

Eldridge dug a chewed yellow pencil into his Weeblefongering. Brother Preston noted with satisfaction the sound of a lead point snapping clean off.

With a satisfied smirk, Preston retrieved Ditto-blue sheets of trigonometry calculations from the greenish braided rag rug (a gift from dear Aunt Livie) and slapped them back onto the desk. Time to get back to Trig. Focusing at the point between his eyebrows, he sent third-eye death rays onto the blank "Write Answer Here" areas. If he stared long enough with the proper concentration level, the homework answers should magically appear.

"Orville Petersen said that's how he does it," Preston grumbled, "but then Orv has an IQ of 382-thousand-somethin and his mom says he does weird yogurt stuff too..."

"GA, idiot-boy, yo-*GAA.*" Eldridge winced as Preston slid into yet another of his infamous malapropisms.

"One *does* yoga, and one *eats* yogurt..." Eldridge suspected Preston malaproped on purpose just to watch Papa George's sparse hair stand up all funny around his bald spot.

Glumly Preston awaited the heavenly bolt of illumination, chin dolefully propped in palms smeared Ditto-blue, elbows planted in desk grooves worn by generations of Gertners.

After a while the monotonous tinka-plink *kachinka*-tink of wintry sleet against their dormer storm windows caused Preston's mind to wander. A tendril of thought that had nothing to do with homework began to slowly form, to writhe its way upward through his bored brain.

"By the way," muttering toward the blanket-shrouded lump hunched over his Weeblefonger, "Do we know anyone gullible? Just think of the stuff you could pull on someone like that. Great stuff— worse'n makinem eat meatloaf. Wouldn't that be great!?"

Silence, followed by the sound of a slowly turning page.

"Hey, *Rubberbutt*, I'm talking at you!"

Lifting one corner of his worn plaid study blanket, Eldridge glared out of his cave of darkness, one eye shooting fire and the other smoldering in blue-brown shadows.

"That's double-mean, Pres! You just better forget about 'gullible' and get back to Trig or there'll be a beating here tonight for sure. A *good*-un!"

Eldridge, whose advantage of two years in age meant he could quite hold his own when it came to the clever and wicked, was suddenly inspired with an even worse infliction.

"Or maybe," he said, drawling out the menacing words, "Maybe they'll forbid you to speed-skate on the lake fer ehhhhhverrrr..." His voice trailed off as the truly ominous prospect of withdrawal of lake privileges registered on Preston's paling face.

"Ah, *sweet* satisfaction," Eldridge mused. "And a proper example of 'gullible,' too. Weeblefonger One, awaaaaay!"

"Keep those eyeballs focused on your education, little mister" he boldly continued. "Ya don't see thunder-thigh big-leggity speed-skaters winning the Nobel in Celestial Mechanics, do ya? And ya know where old 'athaleets' end up around here, doncha? They end up pushin' Ernie's Grab 'n Go Brat Wagons, *that's* what!"

Now, such extra-curricular activities as skating provided rare sweet moments of joy in the Gertner academic regimen. Sporting contests which distracted from one's studies being looked upon as frivolous

3

diversions, quite possibly even a form of scholastic heresy. Speed-skating in particular was likened to "sin on shining blades" by professorial parents, ranking right up there with putt-putt golf and canasta as indulgences one could do nicely without.

But speed-skating on a day with sapphire-bright skies and ice-diamond trees had been a clearly ringing response to "A Prayer in Moments of Profound Desperation" for an energetic Midwestern Lutheran boy like Preston. Breathtakingly fast on the track, he reveled in heady scents of northern woods balsam, the sharp clean bite of ice, and shards glittering in prismic rooster tails behind his flying blades. Ah, the bliss! Ah, the hours spent lake skating by moonlight. "Is this be sin, then count me in!" he had often reckoned, hoping that that didn't cancel out the prayer.

Back at his desk Preston shook his head. "Ya know, a guy could get terminal fidgets from too much study and not enough fun." Working up a good head of indignant fume, "Dad just doesn't know what it's like to be a boy with *needs*!" He heaved a heavy sigh of boy-frustration.

Now having zipped through Trig by expert use of a dowsing string over multiple choice questions, Preston struggled with the very last compound sentence diagram on his own English homework which thus far had not dowsed beyond his dangling participle.

And in the back of his mind, Preston brooded over Eldridge's threat of no lake skating, no outdoor activities. Then that *really* unnerving thought drifted by and slithered in.

"Eldridge said a guy who never gets daylight on his chest won't ever grow chest hair – I'd look like ole Mr. Kruzbacher!" His eyes dilated at the thought.

It was not a pretty sight, Mr. K's chest. Above a jiggling slumping paleness of belly flab, the accountant's bald head and hairless chest came out of hiding each summer at the lake. Preston shivered in a surge of Arctic-cold goose bumps.

Mr. K., peering through glasses thick as a watermelon rind, was wont to disrobe with theatricality tossing a parrot-bright Hawaiian shirt over the family "Drink Blatz Beer" ice chest before striding with dedicated purpose into silken jade waters of Lake Washeegan. He would then roll belly-up (the image of an elephant seal flashed across Preston's mental movie screen) and would commence to bob about, idly paddling as the great bulbous belly absorbed tons of solar radiation. Every year Mr. K. would emerge looking like an immense bulls-eye: a richly roseate tum-tum set off by dead-fish white legs and elbows (the submerged bits), followed by fried red forearms, lobster pink hairy toes and a beaming bald spot. Preston shivered again and focused his third eye really *really* hard on that dangling participle.

After awhile the tree-root sentence diagram began to undulate like a hypnotic belly dancing pendulum. Eyes involuntarily rolled back and he schlumped softly face down into the English textbook. As he slept, "Our Friends the Adverbs" relocated onto his damp cheek as "sbrevdA eht sdneirF ruO."

Sometime during the wee morning hours, in that strange dream-time when restless minds run gleefully amok, Preston's eyelids popped open in a eureka of wish fulfillment. He <u>did</u> know someone "easy, trustful, and naïve," someone round-eyed reeking with gullibility.

"Cousin *Birdlegs*!"

A fiendish grin bulged and widened. Brown-hazel eyes glittered with unnatural brightness in his night-shadowed bedroom. The very thought of tricky forays into that Forbidden Zone beyond Golden Rule boundaries, of being less than a truly proper Gertner gentleman, was utterly dee-scrumpshulicious. And he'd figured out that English problem, too!

And so it became a Wisconsin winter's delight to hole up in the garret and warm heart's cockles with thoughts of the coming August; to lucid dream of the annual Iowa reunion and Uncle Herman's farm outside Hawkeyesville where opportunities

5

abounded to tease and torment the stork-skinny cousin. Musing hours sped at times like these and by summer, ah by summer, a truly Machiavellian, Rube Goldbergian plan could be wrought.

Very careful execution was required to ensure no *obvious* meanness could be detected in The Plan. This prevented hidings (what Uncle Henry termed "applying the hand of knowledge to the seat of wisdom"). Being full of practical Wisconsin academe genes, Preston also understood that to gull one's adversary properly and remain in good standing, one must clearly demonstrate advanced academic achievement to the detriment of the lowly less-learned. One must defeat with Superior Scientific Knowledge, and do it with an innocently straight face without *any* lip-twitching or shoe-shuffling.

Since Cousin Birdlegs was a good three years his junior and in a California school at that, victory was guaranteed.

In the veiling darkness of the Wisconsin garret, Preston beamed beatific. Gone was the looming prospect of yet another toe-curlingly tedious Iowa summer. Dispelled was the bleak sense of limitation, of having no capacity to control one's own world. In the deepness of that moonless January night he cast a hoarded two-week-old selection of unwashed gym socks onto the bedroom floor and read omens of victory in their scattered pattern.

Preston sighed. Eyes dazzled with wicked delight. The Hawkeyesville Boredom Relief Plan was ready.

And so was *he*.

CHAPTER TWO

Birdlegs, oh Birdlegs...

Long ago and far away was a land where a skinny girl went every August. It was a place of strange contradictions, where strict 𝔍𝔬𝔴𝔞 ℜ𝔲𝔩𝔢𝔰 𝔬𝔣 𝔓𝔯𝔬𝔭𝔢𝔯 𝔠𝔬𝔫𝔡𝔲𝔠𝔱 met head-on with her dizzying surges of blissfully unfettered wild-haired California imagination.

To her sense of it all, Iowa in late August was inhabited solely by hallowed skinny-lipped elders who had never never ever made youthful errors in judgment, despite whispers by Great-Aunt Hergwitha about a red hay wagon mysteriously self-assembling astraddle their barn one Halloween.

But just how did Birdlegs get to be "Birdlegs"? Hummm.

It had to have been one of those astrological jokes, or space aliens, or maybe just sweet Grandma Carson's genes from Mama's side of the line, but somehow she was gifted with the most amazing pair of long twiggety bowlegs west of Arkansas.

Now, nicknames presented by family were usually of a kindly tweaking nature with the tacit understanding that one would never be publicly addressed as "Missy

Sillybeans" or "Master Sweetums Funnybottom".

    Playground peers, however, had no such scruples when it came to branding each other with tribal names guaranteed to mortify and laser attention onto one's most embarrassing personal attribute(s). Such monikers as "Beaver-tooth" Mueller, "Four-eyes" Philipoom, or Fitzwalter R. B. "Dribbles" Lautermilch IV had a way of cropping up early and returning to haunt one at reunions or board meetings.

    That Sara Jane Gertner's growth spurt came early on was a heaven sent break for those who reckoned "Little Gigglebutt" was not humiliating enough. There was just something about those knobbly knees which seemed to face sideways rather than the direction her feet were pointing, well they just naturally conjured up "Stork-Girl," "Flamingo Kid," and come winter the "Blue-kneed Bluebird." Eventually, the ghouls of the playground settled on an easier to remember generic. They simply called her "Birdlegs." And so it was.

    Sara suffered in martyred silence, which was the proper thing to do according to the 𝔍𝔬𝔴𝔞 ℜ𝔲𝔩𝔢𝔰 𝔬𝔣 𝔓𝔯𝔬𝔭𝔢𝔯 ℭ𝔬𝔫𝔡𝔲𝔠𝔱 and, more to the point, according to Papa. To overcome spasms of painful shyness brought on by her spindlies, Sara took up ballet lessons twice a week and was assured by a gushing Madam Minette herself that with proper practice Mlle. Sara would one day be a prima ballerina with the most stunning legs in the history of the stage and maybe the world. It was during final rehearsals for their first big evening recital that niggling doubts began to intensify. Maybe ballet lessons *wouldn't* fix the skinny leg thing, much less the bowed knees she was born with. It was merely stage scaredies, Sara told herself, just like she read about in those glossy Classical Dance magazines artfully displayed in the frilly-pink ladies room of Mlle. Minette's. And since no *real* dancer would ever have pre-performance palpations, she too would be courageous -- starting right *now*.

    She took a deep cleansing breath, placed her feet in third position and imagined a string tied to the top of her head pulling her spine into a gracefully straight line.

"It will all pass away the instant I step into those magnificent stage lights. It says so in *Classical Dance*, so it must be a bona-fide-for-truthful fact!"

Head up, chin high, she glided with slowly deliberate ballerina grace toward the stage. She listened for her piano cue then leapt out to meet joyous stardom.

Immediately following what she believed an utterly flawless rehearsal came two hastily convened grown-up conferences: The first between a clearly distressed youth class instructor and the owner of *Mam'selle Minette's Tippy-toe Ballet School*; the second between those elegant ladies and Sara's mother. It seemed there was to be a slight change in costume for dear Mademoiselle Gertner. She would now play a part of greater significance, a *solo* role.

Sara was beside herself with satisfaction. Not for her the guise of a besequined pink-tutu'd purple-tighted cupcake. Elevated to the elite status of Royal Baker, she would soar onto the stage flourishing a long-handled wooden spoon, personally responsible for presenting La Belle Cupcakes to the King and Queen (played by girls at the toe-shoe stage). Oh, and her costume change included *long white pants* and a chef's hat borrowed from Mrs. Gumpster at the deli next door.

That such a change was meant to be face-saving (and knee-covering) did not occur to Sara, being a solo role after all. It was a *promotion*. Mai oui!

It wasn't until the post-recital "giggles and congrats" part of the performance that Sara learned the traumatic truth. When it finally dawned on her that adults chuckling over "that poor thing with the spoon," who apparently "looked just like a sippy straw with the wrapper left on" referred to herself (C'est moi??!!), she determined resolutely to depart the stage forever and become a librarian. She grimly vowed never to do anything solo in front of an audience ever again as long as she lived, Amen twice!

That the ballet calamity came directly on the heels of a junior choir full-house Easter solo when she got brain freeze (forgot the words) and after thirty seconds of dead silence began singing the previous verse two beats faster than the organist was playing...well, the hushed halls of Librarianship looked better and better as a forever career option.

Having a solid career lined up, even though Sara wasn't entirely certain what that meant precisely, seemed very very important to Gertner elders. Whether a kid <u>liked</u> being the world-class expert in Mesozoic coprolite, for example, was way less vital than whether this expertise caused parents to glow brighter than the Mr. Peanut balloon at an Albuquerque hot-air festival. Twas a never-ending fail/pass approval process with scorecards tallied every August at the Hawkeyesville academic pow-wow. Gertners must play academic roles properly, demonstrating quantifiable progress toward success regardless of age or rank. Sara wasn't quite sure how Grandma and the Aunties kept score, but she knew there was a big ante-up in there somewhere with penalties for non-performance worse than finding liver and gooshy lima beans on one's plate.

For Sara, Iowa in August was just part of the yearly cycle, an inevitable seasonal ritual. Winter was zip-up snowsuits with mittens strung up the sleeves and so many layers underneath that she lurched around like a goofy robot.

Spring was a stiffly-new straw Easter bonnet with navy grosgrain ribbons tied under the chin, a shiny quarter for the collection plate, and being squished into boulder-hard pews next to the twice-a-year people.

Autumn was the time for little carved pumpkins lined up on the front window sill, scarlet paper leaves and Halloween make-believe. It was dressing up as a gypsy, or clown, or princess -- whatever could be creatively stitched up with material Mama Mattie had on hand. It was shouting "Tricky-treat!" giggling as miniature loaves of Wonder Bread from the nice man who worked at the factory or crumbly sweet sometimes still warm homemade cookies dropped into cheerfully crayoned lunch bags.

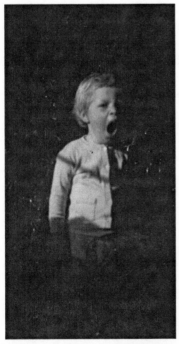

So if it was summer vacation and getting toward late August on the kitchen calendar, Sara could count on corn, cousins, and a sweltering upstairs bunk-bed at the Hawkeyesville reunion.

During the barely-remembered years when Papa still commuted from Virginia through downtown D.C. to the Weather Bureau in Suitland, they spent twenty-three fuel-stop-only hours heading to a map point a tad northeast of Davenport. Sara recalled only leaving at night and arriving at night. After the Federal powers-that-be (and the nice Mayflower moving men) sent them all to the fog-shrouded central California coast, their Iowa trek was merely 2,306 miles of backseat claustrophobia not helped at all by an inability to escape younger brother Roswell, the Furtively Sly. And he *earned* that name.

It was part of the ritual that they always followed official red-lined AAA-approved routes with overnights at the same predestined motels so that after a couple of years brown-aproned waitresses in Winnemucca would comment on how Sara had grown and remember that she hated red onions on burgers. She would also be seated opposite and not next to brother Roswell. Had it not been impolite, bad for business, or too close to where the grey-faced hobos hung out, Marleeneta at the Taste-T Treat Grill in Ogallala would have seated Roswell in a special personal cardboard booth out back in the alleyway.

Roswell was forever whining and never ever happy with what he got. Since what was on everyone else's plate always looked better, which meant that he absolutely *had* to have it, Roswell refined a sneaky snakiness that worked better every time he used it. His technique began with diversionary whining and looking pitiful, devolving into pure poor-me put-upon complete with slumped shoulders and far away pathos in his eyes. That's when sticky fingers would snake goodies into his own pocket. Gertner parents hadn't applied the hand of wisdom to the seat of knowledge early enough. While Mama Mattie and Papa Henry sighed and prayed Roswell would magically grow ethics and honesty given time, they turned a blind eye to a vigorously sprouting bad seed. Given how strict the Gertners were about proper behavior, this turn of events was really confusing to Sara. In fact, she was perfectly aghast at what Roswell got away with and what he seemed to believe was perfectly okay despite blood and thunder admonitions to the contrary from Sunday school teachers and boldly printed "𝕿𝖍𝖔𝖚 𝕾𝖍𝖆𝖑𝖙 𝕹𝖔𝖙'𝖘" in their 𝕴𝖔𝖜𝖆 𝕽𝖚𝖑𝖊𝖘 𝖔𝖋 𝕻𝖗𝖔𝖕𝖊𝖗 𝕮𝖔𝖓𝖉𝖚𝖈𝖙.

Sara decided that some kids were beyond the control of earthly parents. God Himself would have to get her little brother's attention with His big fat karmic paddle. She'd read that could be really painful. The thought made her smile.

CHAPTER THREE

Summer Trekking

It was summer, and time for the Trek to begin. This year's trudge began with bleary-eyed 4:45AM farewells to the familiarity of Carmel Cove sea otters and beloved Mission Ranch horse trails. With a resigned sigh, Sara snuggled under blankets in her designated corner of the back seat, rested a cheek against the frosty window frame and pondered miserably that for three long weeks there

would be no hypnotic surf at bedtime, no sharp clean tang of ocean spray in the air. Worst of all, there would be no horses. In predawn darkness, the monotonous cadence of Goodyear's droning toward Hawkeyesville eased her sweetly swift return into dreamland.

It seemed only moments had passed when the blasting sun of Central California began to bake eyelids onto eyeballs. Sara began to dream in whirling colors of a Technicolor fiesta. She was a day-glow orange tortilla sizzling atop a flat river rock, sliding slowly slowly into white-shimmering bonfires of mesquite. The bonfire was swaying in long languid arcs, as though in a hammock suspended from a sky of many moons. The rolling motion coincided with curves along the California highway, swaying, dipping, rising again ever skyward.

When eyelids eventually unstuck, she dumped the smothering grey wool blanket onto backseat floorboards. Along a sweat-damp cheek, fingers discovered a crimson crease, a streak war paint bright and precisely the width of the Chevy's rear window frame. Then she realized it was really grossly hot in her corner and barfy-belly stuffy. Sara grabbed the back seat window knob and cranked as fast as she could, knuckle-barking for just one breath of freshness. But back seat windows only rolled down halfway and the sultry breeze oozing past her half-awake face merely encouraged a nasty surge of backseat barfs which had been known to be contagious. She glanced over at Roswell. He was still asleep in his corner but looking pale and pink at the same time. Not a good sign. She tapped Mama on the shoulder and quietly pointed to the mini ice-chest. Sucking ice-cubes always seemed to help impending barfs. Feeling relieved and less queasy, Sara turned to get her bearings. Where in the world *were* they???

When Goodyear tires hit shimmering black asphalt bordered by forever vistas of infernally blazing salt flats, it meant you had just passed Salt Lake City. It would be 1:00 P.M. precisely and occupants of the maroon Chevrolet would spend the next ninety-seven minutes dehydrating.

It was agreed that back-seaters needn't be civil, only quiet. The days of warm dog-drool into Papa Henry's pocket protector were yet to come.

One heat relief experiment entailed:

1. DROP ONE BLOCK OF DRY ICE INTO A TURKEY-SIZED ROASTING PAN
2. COVER WITH BLUE SHIRT PAPA WORE THE DAY BEFORE
3. MAKE ROOM ON FLOORBOARD BETWEEN MAMA'S RED-KED-SHOD FEET
4. TURN AIR BLOWER ON BLAST (WORKS BEST WHEN GOING DOWNHILL)
5. CRANK UP WINDOWS, LEAVING WING-WINDOW OPENED ITSY BITSY FOR SAFETY

It was an innovative borderline-scientific experiment. It lasted eighteen minutes. Where Papa Henry found a chunk of dry ice in the midst of a Utah August was one of those cosmic Gertner mysteries one knew better than to question. And Roswell pondered how come Papa's highly honed scientific powers of observation had missed noxious gas tendrils now wisping up from the blue-speckled turkey pan.

Roswell was tops at identifying noxious stuff. In a whispered backseat conference, he detailed to Sara what *could* happen to them as they innocently sped along the brain-numbingly straight roadway across the flats. He made it really gory. As Sara stared at the air around Mama's hair, she decided that guardian angels must be clocking big-time overtime. Clouds of carbon dioxide wafted curlicues through Mama's damp ringlets then streamed out her wing window into a cobalt Utah sky. The stuff didn't keep them any cooler, either.

"Oh, Henry!" Mama Mattie gasped, patting a starched embroidered handkerchief into rivulets of Sable Brown mascara working wiggly trails into her beige pancake makeup.

That comment was soon followed by a muttered, "Dear-Lord-have-mercy," muffled by a fistful of now soggy, funky-brown hanky.

15

Twelve point two minutes later, through tightly pursed "Love That Red" lips, Mama let 'er rip.

"Good GOD, Henry! My feet are either frozen or burnt I can't tell which because I can no longer feel them and I, for one, am <u>well</u> beyond fed-up!" Silence from Papa.

"I mean it, dear." There was still no response from Papa. He was: (1.) focused on driving and (2) not about to voluntarily admit that a perfectly well conceived scientific experiment might be going south.

"Do you hear me Henry?! And I do believe both children have fainted." There was then a phrase mouthed that neither child caught, but Papa paled. Mama didn't let fly with threats – ever!

(Oxford, "threat. Noun. 1 - a stated intention to inflict injury, damage, or other hostile action on someone.)

Papa broke out in chicken skin. There were rumors that Madame Marie Laveau was an ancestress on Mama's side, and one just never knew...

Sara began to feel cross-eyed woozy. Roswell's face pinked up and his eyeballs bulged. His freckled nose wedged into the half-moon opening above the backseat window, angled so that salt-flat winds blew straight up flaring nostrils. His lips flattened wetly against the window pane, steaming up the glass. It was a most alarming site to motorists passing on that side of the Chevy.

"Are you *certain* this stuff doesn't give off some sort of noxious gases like Roswell said? Oh, for heaven's sake..." Mama Mattie was now feeling more than a smidgen queasy and could spot nothing alongside the road to hide behind should she feel an urgent need to lose her prunes.

"It's *fine*, Mama," Papa replied. That was his word, his final word, on the subject. The experiment was *scientific*, after all.

Her fingers gripped the Chevy door armrest, white-knuckled in martyred exasperation. Mama Mattie's mouth began to twitch. Sara thought she spotted a little drool of foam. Then it came. Mama's **Raised Voice with Clipped Syllables**. It was ominous. It was absolutely to be feared.

      "Pull - over - right - now, Mis-ter, and chuck-out-the-blessed-ice!"

There was a stifled gasp of horror from the back seat. Papa's chicken skin morphed in goose-egg sized hives.

Solid objects on kitchen shelves were known to rattle ominously when Mama used that tone. Indeed, the old tin coffee pot had actually hip-hopped right off the stove motivated by the sheer force of her annoyed randomly-firing chi. The Chevy, and quite possibly Papa, might be in real peril from Mama's wrath.

Having the sense to recognize at last when a perfectly logical cooling solution had gone smack-doodle kaput, Papa cranked the steering wheel and slid them onto the sizzling shoulder of the road. As he lofted dry ice waaay out onto the salt-flats, Papa Henry was trying to recall basic chemistry. Would there be an unfortunate (but scientifically interesting) negative reaction to the amalgamation of dry ice and salt? A small hand mashed a silvery circle on the Chevy's steering wheel. The horn's blaring racket knifed into Papa's calculations instantly returning attention to red-smeared scrunched lips and melting rivulets of brown mascara that was the face of his dearly beloved. And was that a little drool of foam he saw?

Notes for future reference:

- Mothers do not respond well to cooking belt-buckle up and freezing belt-buckle down
- Cool air never reaches a back seat
- Pit stops to address biologically-mandated necessities:

 In the Great Salt Lake Desert, there is nothing to hide behind when prunes kick in and Mother Nature urgently calls

 With rare exceptions, pit stops occur only when the Chevy requires fuel. Period. [*As this particular maroon Chevy was capable of spectacularly frugal fuel consumption, riders were required to develop ten-gallon travel bladders and cultivate knee-locking concentration levels a Yogi master would envy.*]

 20-15 Hindsight. Of course no one knew then that Papa had a "factory-installed" three-liter bladder, a medical revelation of later years greeted with "Well, that explains why he never stopped!" from a **still**-annoyed Mama.

In the backseat of the Chevy, Roswell was cranking up the inevitable post-chocolate-ice-cream-for-lunch whine from "his" corner.

"Aw, Dad, everyone else in the *world* has air conditioning, and they go faster'n fifty-five, and *she's stickin' her toe on my side again, Dad!*"

A fudgy pudgy finger dramatically pointed to three centimeters of blue sneaker touching the grey duct tape separating official territories. Keeping parts of one's anatomy within personal airspace was a part back-seaters were required to play by trek tradition. Depending upon the back-seat whine-level, and sensitivity of front seat nervous systems, tradition also provided the response to territorial disputes.

"If you two don't settle down right now, *Papa* is going to put you in the trunk of this car with all the stinky socks and rotten prunes [although this may be an oxymoron] and that *is* where you will stay until we reach the motel! Do you *hear*?!" If this didn't do the trick, Mama always held the ace.

"No more chocolate ice cream for the rest of the trip, *and no swimming pool at the next motel.* Period! And I *mean* it!"

This pronouncement always provided sufficient motivation to be flexible about territorial claims. She meant it.

Sara noted over the years that gas station food was quality consistent from the greying crags of Nevada to the wheat-gilded prairies of Nebraska. Package contents were more likely to originate in a lab than a farmer's field; gastric discomfort generally followed consumption. Audible expressions of such discomfort were not permitted within the confines of the Chevy, or anywhere else for that matter, being a perfectly dreadful breach of decorum. Counting telephone poles helped. If such an emanation occurred it was never to be discussed unless one could rightfully lay blame for the silent deadly upon a passing caravan of old elephants. Roswell was always seeing elephants everyone else had missed.

Along with stops for fuel were stops permitted at places deemed educational by Papa. Educational pit stops were seen as a parental duty which meant one's parent stood by the car door fidgeting, jingling keys, and staring into the sun for the allocated 14.5 minutes. Road pauses included such natural national grandeurs as pink sandstone spires along Bryce Canyon, the Petrified Tree Forest, Mount Rushmore and its gift shop, the Black Hills

JULY 1961

and its gift shop, and the Hawkeyesville Home for the Bewildered where great-great Aunt Bertie once stayed for a while.

20

Educational fare did *not* include armadillo/ iguana/alligator ranches, Mystery Spots, concrete teepees, or the Spectacular Corn Palace, regardless of protests that a child would die a horrible death right there in the back seat should any of these world-class cultural treasures be passed by. Sulking was rewarded with a handful of trunk-hot prunes and threats of withheld Dairy-Queen privileges, both of which were worse fates than dying.

The stifling maroon Chevy swayed and wound upward from blistering bronze flats into a wonder of cool valleys as they threaded through the sky-touching Sierra and Rocky mountains, then down toward an infinite flatness of Nebraska prairie.

There is something that gets into the blood after hours spent peering out a back seat window, occasionally due to gangrene which sets in with a vengeance after eight hundred miles in that Chevrolet. Sara, unconsciously rubbing a nearly dead left bum-cheek, experienced a rising awareness of how really really *different* the country-side was between near-by Here and far-off There. On occasion, her peculiarly Birdlegs logic and reasoning led to impromptu geography lessons.

"But, *Dad*, we can't still be in the United States! I distinctly remember seeing a place like this -- all flat and no ocean -- in *National Geographic* and it was for sure called 'Ukraine" and not "Prague-Wahoo" like that sign just said.

With a tiny sniff of satisfaction, Sara settled into her corner, stiffly folded skinny arms and declared with aloof certainty, "And everyone knows Ukraine is in the kingdom of Upper Patagonia. *Everyone!*"

"'Prague-Wahoo'? No foolin?" Roswell had been preoccupied with making large tic-tac-toe squares on the window with his sweating feet.

"Aw, Dad, don't tell me we missed downtown Prague-Wahoo too?! Gee, we never get to see *nothin'* fun." Sara glanced over at her brother, noting that he was hiding his face so Mama couldn't see just how sarcastic he was being. Mama tugged a much-thumbed red-lined *Rand McNally Road Atlas* from beneath the front seat.

"Now Sara dear, surely you were mistaken. I am certain Prague-Wahoo is in *Lower* Patagonia County."

Papa Henry winced and kept driving. Roswell returned to soggy toe-doodles and apparently saw a really big elephant everyone else had missed. Mama pinched her nose, quietly took the name of the Lord in vain and passed the Rand McNally to Sara.

"Study pages 47 and 48 dear. And Roswell, I believe you need some more prunes. Or perhaps not quite so many dried apricots." Mama had not yet grasped that prunes were the root cause of elephants in the backseat.

"'Nebraska: The Platte River flows eastward through undulating sandstone and loess-covered plains; foothills of the Rockies in the Far West. Principal mineral products: stone, sand and gravel, petroleum, and -- natural gas.'" Sara stared at Roswell.

"I guess you're full of mineral products, Roswell. Mineral products and *prunes*!" (Being "full of prunes" was Mama's special way of telling someone they were full of baloney.)

Firmly motivated by a fresh parental requirement to study all states through which they were passing, Sara endeavored to please by memorizing arcane statistics about Kansas and Iowa. It helped that they were on concurrent pages in the Rand-McNally.

"**Kansas**: Rolling valley-cut plain in East; high, gently undulating plain in West. Elevations increase gradually westward. Zinc, coal, clays, petroleum. Oh no! *More* natural gas!"

Roswell smiled secretively and reached for his hidden stash of prunes. He knew there would be road construction somewhere ahead. There was always roadwork during the summer months. And where there was roadwork, there would be potholes. And where there were potholes, he could let 'em rip when the Chevy bottomed out and claim it was accidental. Roswell always planned waaay ahead for his dirty deeds, preferring the appearance of "incidental and accidental" to the obviousness of intentional. On that thought, he swallowed two extra fat prunes.

As they neared Iowa, Papa's foot inched the gas pedal closer to the floorboards. He was heading home, to his boyhood stomping ground, his siblings, and dear Mama Gertner. He was going to a place where he could get shed of the worries, woes, and hopefully *the children* for awhile. Cold beer. Peace. Quiet. Classical music on the Victrola. Mama Gertner's plain Iowa home cooking (that did *not* include Mama Mattie's favorite Atchafalaya Blend seasoning). All options appeared really first-class.

"It used to take months to get this far, you know." Papa said with Gertner certainty. "Pioneers used to sail across the grassy plains in 'prairie-schooners', great Conestoga wagons with ship's sails mounted atop. Look it up! We are making fantastic progress. *Days* instead of months." He nodded and perked up, suddenly feeling personally blessed that he didn't have to suffer *months* with bored children in the backseat.

Sara too perked up and tapped Papa on the shoulder. "Uncle George said 'such rapid progress from the California coast would have been considered fantastical in that long ago when you and God were boys.'" Papa winced. Uncle George never lost an opportunity for the wry dig. Mama blinked once, then quickly stared out her side window pressing a wadded hanky hard against "Love That Red" lips. She was really trying hard not to burst out laughing. Papa glared, glanced at the dials on the dash then stared straight ahead.

"135 miles till the next gas station." He knew Mama had the bladder capacity of a gerbil.

Roswell whispered from behind his hand, "There were big honkin' dinosaurs then, ya know. Back when God and Papa were boys." Sara's eyes widened at this tidbit of inner sanctum wisdom.

'Really?' she whispered, "No foolin'?' Roswell the Furtively Sly just nodded, stifling a smirk.

"What a brick! Ole Brick-for-brains Birdlegs," he thought. "Say somethin' with a straight face, real innocent-nice, and she'll buy it fer sure 'cause she can't believe anyone on earth would fib big *on purpose*. Jeez, I gotta remember that!"

Sara huddled, concentrating raptly on each new scene, freckled nose flattened against a dust-dimmed window. The possibility that there were true wonders just ahead, just around that next bend, gusted through an already active and fertile imagination. From the first sight of the Great Salt Lake Desert to discovery of mud-flat islands in a gravy-brown Missouri River, she began to consider that the annual trek might actually involve fun. That such intent observations tended to create silence in the backseat was of significant relief to road-weary parents up front.

As they at last reached the outskirts of Hawkeyesville, precisely as the noon whistle on the old firehouse went off, beetle-browed Papa Henry's jaw began to gradually unlock. His lips gradually lost that skinniness which boded ill tidings to anyone silly enough to insist on conversation. After days of strange food and fitful sleep in AAA Bide-A-Wee's, the prospect of actually reaching the farm in time for the reunion began to take on a semblance of reality.

Sara gazed out her window not really seeing passing fields or picturesque villages. She was pondering personal fiascos of reunions past, humiliations which nearly always were followed by a grown-up's patronizing: "It's all right, dear. You're just trying too hard to please" statement of the naturally obvious. It was difficult to live up to lofty Gertner expectations, especially when one tried too hard.

And then there was that inability to anticipate ghastly practical jokes so beloved of Cousins Preston and Eldridge, now aided and abetted by brother Roswell. Gritting her teeth, she vowed "This year will be different. I'm gonna watch them every single minute like a hawk. All of them! And this year, I'm gonna check my Keds for night crawlers *before* I put 'em on, too!"

She stared down at her new sneakers, mentally seeing again a wiggling pinky-brown Mr. Worm and his happy kinfolk peeking out from between her toes. Sara had not been allowed into the house that year until her offending footwear had been well hosed and been inspected for unlucky remains.

Aunt Livie had adamantly refused to allow sneakers smelling of fish bait into her sacred wash. Grandma Gertner, aghast, was certain sure there had to be wee bits of Mr. Worm lurking between toes which would surely "become one" with her best oriental rugs.

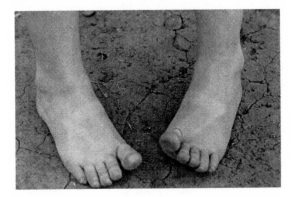

L. Johnston Lewis

In any event, Sara's sneakers could not be discussed at table given that supper that night was meat sauce spaghetti.

Young Master Roswell was banished to the kitchen after staring intently into the bowl inquiring "Mr. Wiggles, is that you?"

Yep. Best to check *twice* this year.

CHAPTER FOUR

Hawkeyesville

For those who through fortune of birth were born into a German-Danish family whose ancestors homesteaded Iowa Territory

in the 1860's, there were but two acceptable lifestyles: eternal academic achievement or farming. Uncle Herman's karmic penance was to pour money into the ancestral acreage until he went broke, so the rest of the clan got Publish or Perish.

" PORP," as Uncle George labeled it, equated one's personal value and status to the count of file cabinets required to house one's published works. There were properly restrained squabbles as to whose lot was worse.

Every August, Gertner professors would trek to Hawkeyesville (population 2,457, somehow all related), to a white late-Victorian on the southernmost edge of town. After all were settled in and settled down, there would be an accounting of the previous year's achievements. Oldest generation siblings would solemnly parade

awards, commendations, and honors for excellence by Grandma Gertner. After all, it was she who set the pace for excellence in the 1920's, being elected the first woman on the County School Board. Later named runner-up Iowa Woman of the Year, she proceeded to take on the raising of five cousins when their parents were killed in an accident. It was agreed that she was one heck of an act to follow.

When phase one of the merit ritual had concluded, iced-tea would be served in the good tumblers and turns taken around the room, based on rank by age, to discuss less weighty matters like the geopolitical state of the planet, latent idiocy in the White House occupant-du jour, and methodologies for successfully raising the next crop of Gertner professors-to-be.

Aunt Livie, who required the term "spinster" be spoken with reverent dignity, would pat a perpetually perfect chestnut chignon, and casually drop that two more of her definitive texts on Child Education were slated for national publication. As a professor of Elementary Education, with thirty years of practice at the same college, Livie was considered the official guru on the subject.

Uncle Herman and Aunt Gert *(never* to be addressed as 'Gertie' on pain of an affliction of the eternal ilk) would follow Aunt Livie with an exhaustive rendition of "This Year's Excitement on the Farm." Such recollections would include the hired boy's unfortunate swim in the manure spreader, a two-headed six-legged Holstein calf, the new still-gleaming attachment for Uncle Herman's best John

Deere tractor, blight, disease, taxes. This was always concluded with "but at least the children are grown and gone, thank God!"

At the proper time, judged by the fidget factor and just before Uncle George and Aunt Minerva, would come a break for iced-tea refills and seventh inning stretch (with discrete rush to the only loo). Protocol dictated that George and Minerva would then regale their brethren and sistren by passionately extolling virtues of life at a major Wisconsin university. It would be passion with a small "p" of course since Gertners firmly believed in *civilized* behavior defined by Grandma as "a stoic detachment that never condones outbursts of pure gut emotion -- happiness, sorrow, or political."

Children were considered deplorably uncivilized creatures until they'd fetched home at least a masters degree in Education, Science or an "–ology." Artsy humanity degrees didn't count unless it could be absolutely confirmed that they were morphing into dignified Engineering or Architecture plaudits. *(Oxford Dictionary: from the Latin plaudite 'applaud!' said by ancient Roman actors at the end of a play.)*

Uncle George and Aunt Minerva applauded the early-on decision of elder son, Eldridge the Inscrutable, to study for the Wisconsin bar.

Minerva announced with pride, "While we agree that ambulance chasing lawyers are gooshy-sleazy creatures, our Eldridge shall be an exception, having chosen to represent our fine American industrialists." She paused for effect, ostensibly to fold the paper napkin in her lap. "He is, of course, the finest orator since Tullius Hostilius. Tullius was with the Roman Republic, you know." Being with a properly intellectual set was of paramount importance to Minerva.

"Dear." Uncle George spoke softly, careful of the personally sensitive landmines upon which he might tread, Minerva having just begun her "change of life" time of hormonal weirdness. "Hostilius was too busy with cattle raids on the Alban border to orate, dear. Besides, Rome wasn't a Republic then. I do believe it was a kingdom." It wouldn't do to be incorrect about ones historical facts in the Gertner household. Someone was *bound* to notice and dance gleefully all over the shortcoming.

"Well, phooey, tooey and phooey again!" Aunt Minerva sputtered. This was her private "You are *really* annoying me, dear" code phrase which Uncle George took for a warning shot across his bow. Her hand began to flutter in twitchy annoyance, edging close to the iced-tea. Knowing its brawny tannic strength would permanently stain whatever it touched, George deftly lofted the tumbler just as the hand of his beloved gusted by, saving trousers *and* the upholstery. Aunt Minerva, not missing a beat, continued her lecture.

"Our Eldridge will be a barrister in the finest tradition - kingdom *or* republic. One can't deny that having gratis legal advice in the family will be well worth the expense of Law School." That Eldridge considered "giving freebies" a character flaw was utterly beyond their comprehension. Eldridge the Inscrutable never openly questioned authority, engaged in distastefully physical competitions, or performed curious experiments on winged insects. He found it preferable to agree absolutely to any request, especially chores, and then disappear off the face of the earth until moments before the hot meatloaf was served.

"That having been said, our Preston's nature is lamentably "outdoorsy." He isn't the studious boy our Eldridge is, you know, and there is that dreadful tendency to dawdle with chores. But," Minerva sighed, wringing her hands, "there is always hope...."

Grandma Gertner leaned forward, one eyebrow slowly raised.

"Minnie, that sounds remarkably like a complaint. Preston is young enough to be properly formed and I am certain that with a *firm hand*, all will be well *in the end*, don't you agree?"

Around the room heads nodded vigorously. It was wise to agree with Grandma, especially when reminded of her favorite adage:

"Civilized persons don't complain. They maintain dignity and by Gott *fix* the problem."

There were concerns that one day Minerva would permanently fix Preston.

Preston the Basher required more diligent prodding if he was to reach required heights of Gertner greatness; his reputation had zoomed south early on. At age five, brandishing a plaster cast on his already busted forearm, he claimed to be the Norse god Thor,

31

letting fly with his mighty hammer-thwacker against Eldridge's kneecaps. Such behavior immediately led to review of known gene pools, including those whispered "peculiar branchings" of the family tree back in the Old Country.

Now, it needs be understood that by hoary family tradition the Gertners were active pacifists and, although Lutheran by pronouncement, they were more Quaker by practice. In the mid-1800's, Carstens Gertner went so far as to leave University in Germany for the New World to avoid serving in the latest killing spree ongoing between nations. Gertners were dairy farmers, and teachers, and educators; warriors of the mind, not militia in the field. Elders strongly emphasized to offspring that "unexpected outcomes oftimes come from a rash rush into emotion. War and violence are never the first answer to issue resolution." That the occasional black eye could oftimes come from being a pacifist on the playground was also an unfortunate fact of life.

Coming full circle around the room, it would at last be Papa Henry and Mama Mattie's turn. They would sigh over the travails of Northern California life: eternal infernal fog, ocean breezes rusting out Chevrolet innards, inflated tourist prices in town. When the subject could no longer be avoided, they grudgingly detailed academic achievements of their progeny: Sara Birdlegs and Roswell the Furtively Sly. Sara quite excelled in the Humanities but needed tutors for Scientific Logic. Roswell did well in every subject; they suspected teachers (or at least test answers) were being bought.

Around the corner from the living room, the uncivilized child-creatures were seated in slumps on the narrow Victorian staircase being neither seen nor heard. For them the annual ritual was a dreadful bore.

Roswell groaned, "Grownups never do nothin' fun. They probably never did nothin' fun when they were *kids*, neither! We're bein' Gertnerized *all the time*."

In doleful agreement, the cousins nodded. It was common knowledge that Gertner parents absolutely for sure had beatific childhoods during which no sin of any kind was performed or even contemplated. (Gertner parents long ago agreed amongst themselves that retelling tales of wagons assembled atop hay barns, or bopping Ole Miz Peeble's hand-fed red squirrels with dried beans sped by slingshots, would be poor examples of Proper Gertner Conduct and certainly lessen their effectiveness as role models. Besides, such stories would surely cause ideas to ferment in prolific imaginations – a condition to be 𝕲𝖔𝖙𝖙 𝖎𝖓 𝕳𝖎𝖒𝖒𝖊𝖑 avoided!)

Of course there *was* that one possibility of an earlier fermentation, a little Gertner secret from the past that Eldridge had overheard. Something about mason jars brimming with wicked-powerful "Lutheran Lightning" hidden in the damp far reaches of the root cellar. Cousins agreed, however, that that story just *had* to be a filbert of someone's imagination because they knew for a fact that elder Gertners, being mostly academics, were physiologically incapable of fibbing. And other than it being illegal and all, they would not have concocted anything so unsanitary and chemically unstable as home-brew anyhow, although Great-Uncle Karlsen *was* half-bald from what he labeled "a youthful medicinal decoction gone unfortunately awry." The cousins exchanged glances. Was it possible? They glanced toward Grandma Gertner. Naaah. The perpetrator would be dead by now for sure. Grandma would have seen to that. Grandma toed the line, and so did everyone else.

33

The cousins waited quietly as possible while the grownup ritual was underway, stuck on the narrow staircase unless and until their "presence was required" in the main show ring. That dreaded commandment boded only misery; twas an event to be scared of.

A Gertner summons could only mean an academic performance was about to occur. The poor stuckee might have to execute mathematical calculations on the fly or regurgitate memorized bits of something classical and ugly-hard, maybe even in a foreign language, while Grandma stared intently and parents probably prayed. Inevitably some humiliating gaffe of the past year would be then be recalled, resurrected, ruminated, and howled over while the victim was stuck in the middle of the circus ring, blushing or, as in Roswell's case, discovering he suddenly had to go number two really really bad.

Awaiting the inevitable summons, the cousins lounged as best they could on the narrow steps as the parlor drone just went on and on and on and on. They were so bored that not even Preston's popping his double-jointed knuckles and knees in time to "One-Eyed One-Horned Flying Purple People Eater" seemed funny.

"Welcome to Hawkeyesville." Roswell whined nasally from his lower staircase perch. Then sensing a captive audience and perfect opportunity, with the tiniest smirk of satisfaction Roswell saw a really skunky old bull elephant. Oblivious up-winders were still humming "Purple People-Eater," counting knotholes in the knotty pine wallboard or measuring how many finger-widths wide the stair tread was when Eldridge, whom Fate had seated nearest Roswell downwind, suddenly turned dead frog green and bolted for the front porch. On his heels, the remainder tip-toed really fast praying grownups wouldn't see them and that no one let the screen door slip and slam.

Back in the parlor, Aunt Gert turned to Uncle Herman, nodded toward the kitchen and whispered "I think one of us should double-check the lunch chicken. Something is pooky back in that direction." She sniffed again, then pinched the tip of her nose.

"*Really* pooky!" she hissed.

Having just caught the word "pooky," Roswell, now with the whole staircase to himself, smirked big. Ah, *success.* One made one's mark in the world with whatever talents one possessed. And Roswell the Furtively Sly still had *plenty* of elephants up his sleeve.

Later that afternoon, the bored cousins were comparing notes when they realized that respective parents were highly consistent in verbal admonishments toward better behavior. More than coincidental turns of phrase, the admonitions were dead spot on exact. It just *had* to be collusion. There had to be a secret Dr. Spock phrasebook or Government pamphlet somewhere which laid out mandated speeches. It just wasn't possible for every adult to be spouting the exact same phrases without some sort of Cliff Notes.

Just for hoots, the truly courageous and brazen made up a game. Hearing the beginning of a rote phrase, they planned to just go ahead and fill in the blanks with an Oxford-Gertner standard retort. For example, Uncle George might start:

"With your <u><<insert Oxford-Gertner Standard phrase here>></u> like that, I don't know how you will *ever* "pass that Trig test" or "...reach your 13th" or "leave the house before you're fifty."

To complete the <<insert here>> phrase, Eldridge might preemptively insert: "ability to tell time," "unbelievable appetite," "appalling study habits," "language," or "manners." If he totally lost his mind and in a rush of effluent to the brain thought he could outrun Papa George forever, he would go-for-broke with all time biggies: "attitude," "hygiene," or the bad words that just made his Dad's head do a 180° spin whilst sputtering "*What did I just hear you say to your Mother*?!" The game sounded like great fun at the time, with endless possibilities.

"I don't know about at your house, but at our house when Mom and Dad are really tired and not happy with our behavior," Preston puckered his mouth and took on a British accent, "They go polysyllabically Oxfordized, like: "You are being unreasonably and irascibly acrimonious to your Mother!" or 'Your egregious insubordination is intolerable!'"

What he didn't share was what followed such a pronouncement -- punishment by shunning or Gertner Braille (the hand of wisdom thwacked thrice upon the seat of knowledge). The coup de grace was an inevitable trip to the Oxford Unabridged to be viewed standing up, of course, as was prudent following the hand of wisdom exercise. Eldridge the Inscrutable later claimed that he purposely used that method to extensively enlarge his vocabulary.

Ritual presentation of a gift-wrapped engraved Oxford on one's thirteenth birthday, as if the obvious could be disguised by rocket ships or romping bunnies, was likened to a Bat Mitzvah rite of passage, Gertner-Lutheran style (no dancing). For the cousins, the occasion marked a milestone of a different sort. It publicized the astonishing fact that they had actually survived to *reach* a thirteenth birthday.

CHAPTER FIVE

The Sacred Kite & Other Mysteries

"There is something metaphysical about a kite in full flight. Tethered to earth by a mere bit of twine, it only appears to be manmade. When Wind breathes life onto its wings, the creature soars, tugging toward invisible stars in the morning sky. It catches the rhythms of life borne upon the spring breeze and its whirling dance is of freedom. It is said that when a truly great kite breaks its tethering string, when it is so high against the sky that you can no longer truly see its shape, then it is touched by the Immortals and, like Pinocchio, becomes real. If it loves you, the kite will return with blessings on its wings."

Cousins Eldridge, Roswell, Preston, and Sara were seated cross-legged on Grandma"s newly mown side lawn, mouths open in awestruck wonder at Papa Henry's tale of the Sacred Kite floating high and serene above. Papa Henry had a knack for making the mundane seem quite miraculous.

Winking at Uncle George, Henry brought forth from his pants pocket a small blue notepad and four stubby No.2 pencils.

"Would you like to send a message to the Sky Immortals? Write something on this," he said, ceremoniously handing each child a pencil and a single blue-lined page. "Fold it just so, and when you've finished, hand it back to me for Sending Up." The kids huddled over their work, seriously pondering what was appropriate to say to a Sky God, something that wouldn't get them struck by lightning for being impudent.

Eldridge had covered one side of the paper and was well into the reverse when Uncle George dryly opined, 'It needn't be a monograph, son. This is supposed to be *fun.*"

One by one the cousins dropped their hopes and dreams into Papa Henry's outstretched palm. Carefully tearing one side of each sheet, he slipped them onto the taunt twine, deftly transformed their shapes into little cones, and let go. Brisk winds filled the papers and in moments messages were being whisked along the string high into the August sky. The children giggled in nervous delight, excited but unsure what would happen next. Note after note was slipped onto the twine line to the Sacred Kite, flying now on nearly five-hundred feet of tether and with a tail close to twenty-five feet long. Aunt Gert would later grump about the shredding of the better cotton sheets, Sacred Kite or no Sacred Kite.

When the spiral notepad was finally bereft of pages on which to scribble wishes and messages, the Kite seemed to sense that all had been said. With a tug of surprising strength it shot up into a passing cloud and left Papa Henry with only two feet of twine dangling in his hand. While everyone else bewailed the loss of their magnificent Kite, Papa Henry merely scanned the sky and measured the wind with his eyes. Bolting into the old yellow farm truck, he took off like a rattling rocket down the dirt road in the direction the Kite was last seen drifting.

In what seemed merely a brief hour, although Henry would claim it was much longer, the dusty Ford pulled back into the drive with a triumphant Kite-Master at the wheel. From the hidden depths of the truck bed he lifted the magnificent, although somewhat bedraggled, five-foot Kite complete with tail and a handful of battered twine. Had it not been a heathen thing to do in front of the neighbors, the cousins would have bowed down to its Sacredness.

Papa Henry explained, "It's merely a matter of understanding meteorological phenomenon and spatial relationships. For example, a paper kite weighted down with X amount of cotton twine and tail moving in a constant breeze will generally drift in such and such a direction only for Y amount of time." There was an awed silence.

The cousins disagreed. They were quite certain the Immortal's Kite had returned out of sheer love of Papa Henry. Period.

Even Aunt Livie was stunned. "It does seem extraordinary that he should have gone directly to the correct cornfield, and that the kite should have landed on a split rail fence right by the side of the very road he had taken. " After all," she glanced over librarian half-spectacles at other Gertners lingering on the front porch steps, "*Eight miles* of cornfield and pasture is quite a bit to cover, what with breezes and roads not always going in the same directions and all..."

Murmuring among themselves, they pondered the awesome possibility that dear Henry might be a True Magician...

Papa Henry enjoyed amazing family with this uncanny ability to visualize outcomes. A special treat, especially for Cousins Eldridge and Preston who prided themselves on logical thinking, was the matter of the Chinese wooden puzzles. Those were the frustrating little balls, squares, and heptagons which only the very young can reassemble with ease because they don't know it can't be done. Every year the boys would ferret out a particularly complex puzzle, disassemble it in private and then spread the pieces on the ritual card table in an utter jumble. The old kitchen timer would be set, Papa Henry would be given a clue as to the original shape of the object, and everyone would stand back. Every year he astonished his audience.

Usually in less than five minutes on the ticking timer, Henry would have completely reassembled the beast, without error and without exchanging one piece for another at any time during the procedure. He simply visualized how each piece would have to be placed in order to construct the whole. Modestly, he never acknowledged that such a feat was beyond the ability of 99% of the population of Earth. It was merely a demonstration to encourage young folks to undertake the *seemingly* difficult.

It was years before the cousins grudgingly acknowledged that they were part of the unwashed 99% as far as Chinese puzzles were concerned. They resigned themselves to hand games for which the only requirement was the ability to get six mini ball bearings into six even smaller cardboard holes.

And Papa Henry loved toys. Whimsically clever toys. The cousins could count on his coming up with at least one truly amazing entertainment each year. Once it was a windup blue octopus that

walked right up the dining room wallpaper on rubber suction cups glued to tentacle ends. And since he especially liked gizmos that demonstrated Scientific Principles, there was the miniature steam engine fired by sugar cube-like blocks doused with lighter fluid slipped under a shining black boiler.

Cousin Preston was particularly intrigued by that toy to the consternation of elders who promptly hid the lighter fluid.

Since Grandma refused to have one of those new-fangled television sets in her house (she was quite certain that watching it caused brain death and blindness), having Papa Henry and his gadgets guaranteed cousins at least an occasional evening of enormous fun. The usual alternative to evening boredom (listening to parlor Gertners discuss the state of the universe and whose tenure was up for review) was hanging out on the front porch.

Through the streetlights danced gnats, moths, and lumbering Iowa mosquitoes. And out of the night sky (and from Grandma's attic where several had taken to nesting) would swoop swift brown bats. Squeaking₁ feasting with abandon, they would skim open-mouthed through the bug sea beneath the beams, much to Roswell's delight.

Sara generally observed this nightly display with a wire mesh basket over her head, having been assured by Cousin Eldridge that bats liked netting in braids better than eating bugs, *any day!*

Papa Henry's uncanny abilities had long since earned awed respect. There was the tale of how he taught himself to read. When the aunts and uncles were still were children, Grandma would gather them around her in the parlor after evening chores and read wonderful stories in German. Most families in Hawkeyesville still spoke a dialect of their old language until well into the 1930's. With perches on Grandma's chair already occupied by older siblings, Papa Henry would stand quietly before her, peering over the top of the book. The day the schoolmarm, Miss Henderson (nicknamed 'Old Blister Britches' by her students), handed Henry a McGuffey primer and asked if he knew a word or two, the inmates of the schoolhouse realized that there was a marvel amongst them. Henry had shyly glanced toward Mrs. Henderson, carefully turned the primer *upside down* and proceeded to read the entire page - perfectly.

This talent for doing the unexpected -- perfectly -- continued. There was the legend of the famous impromptu golf game between

L. Johnston Lewis

Uncle George and Papa Henry. Neither realized that rental clubs only came "right-handed." Now Papa Henry was a southpaw. Feeling neither discouraged nor handicapped, however, Henry heaved a sigh as they teed up then played all nine holes under par - with a mashie.

CHAPTER SIX

Birdseed Birdlegs

Finding spaghetti on the Hawkeyesville menu was as great a culinary oddity as being handed a fresh Manhattan bagel loaded with lox, capers and Bermuda onions on the way out to the hay-baler. Family members might risk taste bud exposure to non-Iowa cuisine on their own time, but here at the Home Place traditional fare was expected and required. Let spaghetti onto the Hawkeyesville menu and next thing one knew there would be

bangers and mash, Carolina barbeque, chow mein, Baton Rouge gumbo, tossed salad with cashews, pink flower petals, or sheep eyeballs nested in wild rice staring one in the face.

No, Iowa fare was meant to be farmer's fare: homegrown, hearty, starchy, plain, and preferably from a cookbook printed in Old German or on 3x5 recipe cards handed down through the generations.

This is not to imply that experimentation was verboten. After all, occasionally there was a practical need for luxurious cream sauce upon items in need of disguise or stretching.

Sara couldn't stand mystery food. One should never be so stodgy and fixed in one's ways as to ignore something new. It's just that something new usually turned out to be a creative mix of several something's old, borrowed, bottled, or blue. Although days of pre-dawn farm chores and the necessity for tables groaning beneath the weight of a personally produced cornucopia were but a memory, tradition declared that the tables still groan when diners arrived, and diners happily groan when departing the table.

Dinner or "supper" -- Sara could never remember which was in reality lunch -- always consisted of corn, another veggie (peas, carrots, rutabaga, or something odd creamed into obscurity), a huge bowl of potatoes, some form of animal life (generally a hapless chicken), fresh breads loaded with local creamery butter and honey, Grandma's pickles, umpteen salads, and of course, dessert. Steaming homemade apple pie with raisins, mince pie [raisins], cherry pie with raisins, carrot/sweet potato pie with raisins, rhubarb pie (regularity being a Godly attribute) and - occasionally -cake, with raisins. Such diet was guaranteed to replace tonnage lost during the taxing trek to Iowa, to provide one with healthy apple cheeks and an intimate familiarity with the gravity-fed wall-mounted pull-chain porcelain loo upstairs and to your left.

The scent of Uncle George's experimental spaghetti sauce wafting from the kitchen was an event necessitating immediate investigation. Tentatively lifting the black cast-iron lid with a quilted calico potholder, Sara stretched on tippy-toe, bent over the steaming cauldron, inhaled deeply of the rich aroma, and sneezed. Fortunately not directly into the sauce.

It was one of those whimsies of Nature which brought an August breeze slipping over the windowsill to puff lightly across that particular bowl patterned in Old Roses. A bowl filled plumb brimful with fluffy golden shells and tiny amber seeds. Specifically, the leftover birdseed from Saint Peter Parakeet's dinner (supper?) bucket.

The untimely combination of errant breeze and Sara's rather forceful snort caused a golden flurry over the deep enameled sink and old white stove. Golden shells fluttered like fairy dust amid streaming sunbeams, then came to settle gently upon a sea of bubbling crimson sauce. Sara was stunned - as much from experiencing intimate contact across the toes with a clattering cast-iron lid as from the sight of a desecrated dinner.

Beside the sink an antique brown crock sprouted a nice selection of long handled wooden spoons. Sara fastened fingers around a really big one and proceeded to furiously stir St. Peter's pre-pecked parcels into saucy invisibility.

St. Peter was the sole "animal" allowed to reside within the house, the commonly held belief being that cats, dogs, bent snakes, and limping crows were "outside" creatures. It was a fact of life that critters that didn't pull their weight around a farm were luxuries. It was also a painful lesson of life that one could not attach too much sentiment to any critter lest one have to deal with the travail of Fluffy appearing with garnish on the dinner table. St Peter was the grudging exception, having been won at the Scott County Fair years back by a boy unable for parental reasons to transport it home to Wisconsin.

To the astonishment of progeny, Grandma graciously agreed to give Saint Peter a trial run with the understanding that if he proved an unsatisfactory companion, one could expect to receive a pre-tested recipe for parakeet pie.

And despite Saint Peter having learned to brilliantly mimic her particular ring on the hand-cranked wall-mounted central-operator telephone, followed by a screeching series of raucous nasal "Hello? Hell-ooOOO's?" he was still blithely pattering about his perch the following summer.

With St. Peter chiming in the background, Sara stirred until nary a shell could be spotted. Then inspiration hit. If bird seed was so good for the sainted Pete, then it was probably really good for people as well. Why else would there be a bowl full of the stuff right by the stove if not for use in one's cooking? And if a little was good...

Sara replaced the empty bowl neatly back upon the windowsill, humming with pride at her cleverness. What a help she was in the kitchen. Wouldn't the folks be pleased? Oh happy *happy* day! Not that she would let on that she had doctored the spaghetti sauce...

"Let's just wait and see their eyes open wide when this stuff hits their gums. Wowser! Are these guys in for a treat," she beamed.

Brushing sun-streaked brown wisps back from a perspiring freckled face, Sara happily puttered and stirred until Uncle George appeared with fresh garden herbs to add to his special treat. At his suggestion that she might want to neaten up before dinner, Sara retired to the upstairs facility, comb firmly in hand to tame the unruly bangs. The long braids had disappeared during the winter, being replaced by a neat Prince Valiant bob. With the weight of the braids removed, however, a fierce cowlick had sprung to life towering smack in the middle of her crown. It would not be tamed, not even with water on the comb.

Spying a small jar at the sink's edge, Sara had another bright idea. This was the stuff the boys used to keep their "butch" haircuts standing up arrow straight and neatly stiff. Dipping into the jar, carefully extracting on fingertips what seemed an appropriately sufficient amount, she pressed the slickery goo against her forehead and with a flourish swept it back into the cowlick.

It worked.

The crown of her head sported nary a wisp and the cowlick had been pomaded into submission. According to the mirror, however, there were now distinct furrows plowed across her scalp the same distance apart as goopy teeth of a comb which belonged to fastidious Aunt Livie.

Ignoring titters of Cousins Eldridge and Preston, Sara glided with ladylike grace to the table, anticipating that personal culinary glory to come would cause the sight of her furrows to fade from memory.

It wasn't so much when the sauce hit the gums, as when molars crunched something which generally wasn't supposed to crunch, that startled glances flickered around the table - carefully avoiding eye-contact with Uncle George lest what the diners had encountered was in there on purpose. Sara's self-satisfied grin began to falter and sink in a direct ratio to the increased hard swallows and strangled coughs.

Uncle George lifted a paper napkin to his lips, coughed once then deliberately laid a fork cross-wise at the top of a heaping plate. It was the polite Gertner sign for "all done."

"Excuse me, all. Something has apparently gone amiss with the recipe..."

Pointedly searching the faces of one urchin after another (using The Look to great effect), he worked his way around the table coming in due course to a furrow-crowned lump of misery attempting to liquefy and discretely slide under the table.

Clearing his throat, Uncle George's voice boomed across the table, at least to Sara he sounded as loud as a boom box. George thought his voice was actually rather well modulated, considering...

"Miss.....*SaraJane?*"

All eyes swiveled in her direction. Those of her parents fastened with horror, increased by the realization of something extraordinarily queer about her hairstyle. Those of her cousins lit up in soulful relief at having been spared. Papa Henry leaned back in his chair, stared toward the ceiling, and wheezed "OhdearGod..."

Two eternal hours later, long after the rest of the family had substituted cold chicken leftovers for "Tuscan Spaghetti Bliss" and departed for their evening walk, Sara sat miserably alone at the table munching Saint Peter's spaghetti sauce. All of it. Cold. Right down to the bottom of the shell-encrusted green crockery bowl.

Mama Mattie had insisted this was the only proper way to proceed, all the while muttering, "--and those poor starving refugee babies who would be happy just to have a tiny bit of what's on your plate right now. Well, perhaps *without* St. Peter's birdseed, but nonetheless, young lady, I hope you have learned a valuable lesson..."

Outside, below the open dining room window, Cousins Preston and Eldridge scrunched behind concealing leaves of blue hydrangea.

"Hey Birdlegs," a voice snickered through the window screen. "Mr. Bloemke's got fifty-pound sacks of wild warbler feed on sale. You interested?"

The taunt was followed by the distinctive snapping sound of hydrangea stems as cackling cousins fell into Grandma's favorite shrub. The next sounds were startled wails as her stalwart Iowa walnut walking stick connected smartly with bare shins and olive-drab corduroyed backsides.

It was years before Sara could chew over the idea of spaghetti dinners and even longer before elephant-memoried cousins quit taunting screeches clearly reminiscent of the old telephone's particular ring.

Some time later, making lemonade out of life's lemons, Sara did risk using "Chanson du St. Pierre" to earn a Camp Fire Girl merit bead.

Camp Wikigumee counselors were stumped, I mean *really* stumped, as they closed their eyes and listened intently to Sara's soaring warble-whistles. They couldn't even come close to identifying the critter she had imitated, but figured in all fairness they'd hand over a coveted merit bead anyhow. After all, Miss Sara Trail-seeker had worked really hard for promotion to Wood-Gatherer status, and likely had strained a gusset on that last high trill.

Counselor Sparrow-Sings-Too-Early turned to Counselor Buffalo-Dewgrass as they walked back from the evening's woodland ceremony.

"'Hawkeyesville MaBell' bird? Isn't that what she called it?" Shaking his head, Sparrow-Sings finally had to say what was on his mind.

"That birdcall's bouncing on my brain, Dewgrass. Danged if it didn't sound like Old Doc Hooper's crank-box wall phone. You remember, the one AT&T had to pry off the wall when rotary dials came in?"

49

" 'Hawkeyesville MaBell'. We gotta look that up in the field guide. Do you suppose it's some sort of magpie?" His eyes twinkled. "Or just a complete fakeroonio?"

They grinned. It wouldn't be the first time they'd awarded beads for ingenuity and sheer brass.

CHAPTER SEVEN

Grace and Warts

Summer was over for another year and Sara was facing a crisis. Despite protests that she *preferred* being a wallflower resigned to and destined for a life of dumpy grey granny dresses and hair skinned into a tight bun skewered with a No. 2 pencil, her parents grimly persisted trying to cultivate social graces and boost her self-confidence.

"Girls who are graceless at your age have been known to develop warts *in conspicuous places* later on," dear Aunt Livie advised, and she *was* the family guru on such things.

"A girl *must* practice her etiquette with diligence, or she'll get a bottom of the barrel husband!" solemnly advised Mrs. Hemphill across the street. 'Then everyone will know she dawdled instead of danced at her lessons."

"Get crackin', young lady!" admonished Great-Uncle LeRoy. "Your parents are payin' good money to train you up right. Don't you be bringing shame on the family now!"

And of course grown-ups *never* told fibs or made stuff up to scare the beejeesus out of a kid. Sara thought that they were somehow trying to be encouraging, or at least she hoped so. It was obvious that the business of getting social graces was going to be especially painful for a shy person.

There were music classes. Sara serenely advised Papa that she had chosen the elegant violin as a proper avenue to lyrical grace. After all, violinists were clearly transported into rarified realms of cosmic bliss soon as soon as they picked up that long stick thing with the white hairs. Sara had observed on Ed Sullivan's show that lady violinists always got a far-away look in their eyes; they were supremely self-confident, lyrically composed. Violinista's were elegant, serene, and their legs were always *always* swathed in black-skirted invisibility. For someone with bowlegs, this was a key point.

Mama and Papa exchanged wide-eyed glances at the violin request. Papa Henry's nervous system began to twitch, pre-reacting to the prospect of stomped-on-a-cat's-tail screechy practice sessions right next to his study, not to mention expensive master lessons stretching for oh decades. Ka-ching, ka-ching. Ka-ching. His mental cash register immediately registered an unanticipated negative cash flow.

It was a well-used accordion that sank into Sara's pink chenille bedspread the following Thursday. Hunkered there, it was a sinister lump about as elegant as a cane toad with a full load of swamp booty. With a gazillion buttons littering one side, greyed keyboard and thick worn leather straps, it was a conspicuous declaration that Sara should never ever expect to attain violin-grace. Hanging heavily against her chest, the box felt like penance for every perceived or imagined personal shortcoming, mainly her legs. She dutifully lugged the toady oompah-pah-pah to lesson after lesson, lining up for recitals standing next to the dulcet-toned violin-kids. It couldn't get much awfuller. But it did.

Mama had neglected to share that when she was *en pischouette* (a little girl) playing along side Baton Rouge bayous, anyone who fetched along an accordion when friends made the *vay-yay* (gathered to chat), ma cher, it a good thing was!

But belle Sara wasn't in Le Bayou country. She was in Le Miseryville. Trying to play accordion was for her a pure *pain pee po* (useless activity).

"*Je suis de'pouille,*" Sara moaned. "I am a mess!" And as she felt, so the music sounded.

Weekly lessons dragged on and on through the winter. She could have hung a couple stable anvils around her neck and beat them with silver tie-rods for all the joy the accordion brought. Squeeze-screech squawkety-squack.

"Same difference." Sara grumbled, dragging her torture device to yet another session with the creepy instructor.

"Anvil = toady-box. Toady-box = anvil. I'll never get it right."

Although excruciatingly shy, Sara's abysmal accordion skills eventually led to assignment (here's where it gets awfuller) as the official Little Mistress of Ceremonies. She was to make clever introductions and perky between-performance small-talk for all remaining recitals. Every single one.

Coming from a classic Gertner upbringing where studious silence was the preferred state, having to stand before an audience of peers and grownups making perky speeches...well, there just wasn't a best way to describe the brain pain.

Mama was at first startled, then really really annoyed to find Sara's "toady-box" in the dirty clothes hamper under Roswell's thrice-worn (for good luck) BVD's.

"Ungrateful. That's what she is. Perfectly good musical instrument touching Roswell's skivvies. However can I take this back to the rental store now!" Mama muttered and spat for three days, then glared daggers for the next three. On the seventh day she rested.

As befitted the new role as LMC, Mama went shopping for Sara's special new dress. Pink-checked with lots of pleats, it had a perilously deep scoop front that threatened to expose more than Sara's t-shirt if heaven-forbid she bent forward to retrieve a dropped recital program instead of doing a lady-like back-straight curtsey.

In the store's fitting room, Sara just stared at herself in the mirror. All she could see was ribs and chest. And skin. She absolutely could not make her feet move, or bring herself to walk beyond the faded green dressing room curtain out into the shop where *anybody* could see.

Mama stood in the anteroom just outside the curtain. As passing minutes accumulated with Sara yet to make an appearance, she began to drum her fingers on the wall in mild annoyance. Finally a firm hand reached in, grasped Sara's wrist and drew her forcibly out into the blazing fluorescent lights. Sara blushed cherry pink. Her eyes begged what her mouth could not utter. She just stared at Mama, then down at her chest. From her vantage point, Sara could clearly see t-shirt. Lots of t-shirt. And beyond.

Mrs. Ingersol, owner of "Ingrid's California Boutique," alertly discerned the nature of young Sara's dilemma even if Mama had yet to grasp its significance.

"Not a problem, my dear." She smiled and strode briskly toward the front of the store. "Miss Sara, I believe there's a very nice piece of white pique over here in Remnant Corner, and some sweet cotton lace that would blend beautifully with the bodice of that little dress." A modesty insert was hastily crafted and tacked into the décolletage.

"Bless you to bits." Sara said softly to Mrs. Ingersol while the insert was pinned into place, a bit of tear in her green hazel eyes. Mrs. Ingersol nodded, gently patted her arm, and smiled like the Madonna she was.

"Merci boucoup, Mama," Sara whispered, staring at the pavement in embarrassment as she slid into the Chevy. "It's a lovely dress. Thank you for getting it for me. I know it will look really nice on stage." At least she would look really *swell* when she started to stutter during those odious violinist intro's.

Piano Lessons. Sara would really make an effort this time. *Anything* to avoid warts or another parentally selected torture device. By now discouraged and certain sure of impending disaster, Sara did scales and beginning chords on the handsome upright piano only when utterly alone. Unable to make logical sense of squiggly piano sheet music notations (any more than for the terrible toady-box), Sara defiantly lifted her chin, trusted to intuitive glittering musical prowess (or a past-life as Chopin) and played by ear.

It didn't take long for nice Mrs. Philipoom to report to Mama that her child's ear was tuned to a key that no known piano or musical score even vaguely supported. And her little fingers were too short to make more than a modest 8-key reach. Instead of comforting Sara with the knowledge that she had "hands for playing Mozart," the piano lessons abruptly ended. Mrs. Philipoom returned to more gifted, exquisitely long fingered students, and the upright was replaced by a tasteful Danish Modern sideboard.

Ballroom Dancing. Oh gad. Just awfuller and awfuller. Torturous "Ladies and Young Gents Cotillion" classes were held at the only hotel in town. With crumbling Art Deco architecture and peeling school-bus-yellow painted stucco walls, the Grand Hotel San Gabriela was well on its way to the Historic Preservation "Rescue-me" list or shopping mall conversion featuring a gaggle of gargoyles leering over its sunset-facing entrance.

Since this was long before dance was considered a sport requiring 5" spike heels and wafty-drafty tendrils of feminine attire, Sara dutifully donned sturdy suntan-colored nylons and a yet another frock Mama Mattie had selected from the three at Ingrid's suitable to her string-bean measurements.

Ballroom quickly became more painful than ballet, being co-ed with the nerdliest boys mid-pubescence could produce. Jug-eared, beak-nosed, chinless, and short. Very short. Sara was grateful she'd not yet sprouted a chest like Grenadina Schwartz since that was by far the boy's preferred nasal nesting site. There were fleeting moments when Grenadina was swung around the dance floor in ¾ time that her largesse would bring on a slack-jawed nearly hypnotic focus from her partners. Sara did –but only once!- consider spreading honey on her chest and praying for bees.

"One-two-three, one-two-three, dip-two-three, spin-two-three. This is not a wrestling match, Master Arnold Plotzero," the instructress haughtily informed a struggling young man in unfashionably nerdy tweed trousers.

"One does not *grapple* one's partner. One *flooowwsss* like a little *breeeze...*" Arnold would later become an Alamogordo nuclear physicist which did not require an ability to emulate little breezes or suffer cadet-short haircuts. And he did muster up courage enough to propose to Grenadina.

Tennis, music, cotillion classes. It was all a blur, except for the Ladies Club Afternoon Tea when Sara (with pearls) was first exposed to sugar tongs and spent ten tense minutes micro-scooping granular sugar into a teetering antique Minton bone-china teacup. It was

Mrs. Shanner who lifted first an eyebrow and then the lid on a daintily painted bowl containing square sugar, indicating that the tiny engraved silver spoons to the right were proper for *granular* and only cubes were tonged. It was hard to concentrate on such details when one was trying not to sweat or boggle the Minton.

  Then there was an educational live theater play starring Joe E. Brown, in the company of her parent's best friends and their similarly stork-skinny young son. After a rousing performance, with oodles of one-liners that made grown-ups laugh and then become wistful, Sara accidentally splashed the world's ripest special-purchase dime-store perfume onto the Buick's backseat which resulted in a rapid out-of-town sale.

  What Sara did best was now more often done out of parents line of sight or ear-shot. As often happens to girls her age, she discovered the worlds of *Black Beauty* and *Misty of Chincoteague* at the community library. From then on it was *out* with Egyptians, dinosaurs, and the Count De Saint Germaine and *in* with horses, horses, horses.

It wasn't long before she began to explore past Walter Farley on the bookshelves and discovered a real live public stable just over the Little League field fence and downhill behind the Carmel Mission. It was both haven and heaven to Sara. Ever resourceful, and in ardent need of that $2.50 for an hour of trail-ride freedom, she threw herself into entrepreneurial gigs: babysitting, dishwashing, weeding, and girly odd-jobs around the neighborhood.

Ah the blissful bouquet of horse scents, the sovereignty of the trail!

Stable owners had it all figured out. They could get local girls at the horsey-stage to take tourists on trail-rides *and* pay for the privilege of doing it. Roger-dodger, whaddadeal!

Eventually mastering English, Western, and a peculiar self-taught side-saddle (but no fence jumping, at least not on purpose) Sara made it past the Mission Ranch's three level of confidence tests and was entrusted with seasonal clientele. Considering her youth, this responsibility was a kudo of the first water. She felt the first faint stirrings of pride and self-confidence.

Leading a lurching line of riders whose abilities ran to the extremes, Sara chirped, "Heels down, elbows in, folks!"

Circling back to those in obvious need, or experiencing tender body parts, she encouraged and cajoled until most of the group was up to an elegant canter. Over starlight white sands rhythmically soothed by swells shading celadon green to jaybird blue, they loped and trotted. It was truly bliss.

It was during an otherwise pleasant early morn outing that the cinch strap worked loose on Ole Bucktooth - again. A lumbering chestnut charger reserved for the most timid or girthsome, Ole Bucktooth had recently developed a liking for bloating his belly during cinch-up with a later discrete exhalation that would allow saddles to slop around real nice and loose. Bucktooth's regimen, along with the bloat and regardless of who was up top, also included a leg-stretching run on packed sand at the ocean's edge. With any luck, and a novice rider, he could bolt blissfully free, half-barrel roll into tinkling-cold surf, and generally thoroughly trash every inch of leather tack. Although innocence glowed warm in chocolate-dark eyes, there was mischief times two on Bucktooth's mind.

On this pale early Sunday morn, after exhaling and blowing a satisfyingly loud alfalfa-scented wind, he had set his mind on a good solid run perhaps polishing it off with a log-leap at the far end of the white sands. As the line of riders passed out the main stable gate and wound up Beach Lane, Bucktooth began working the bit around until he had a good solid bite. His tourista-du-jour, whose last riding experience had been a childhood birthday dappled pony, was death-gripping the saddle horn while reins, wadded into a squishy ball, lumped in her lap. She was having a hard time "finding her seat" as Sara had coached. The new sea-foam blue cotton slacks from "Seaside Togs" were sliding in ever greater pendulum swings -- a most unladylike motion for a Charleston matron. But then, she anguished, in order to hold reins she would have to release either a fistful of mane or the saddle horn, neither of which seemed reasonable courses of action.

"Sit straight, heels down, comfortably holding reins in one hand while gently directing your mount." The young voice carried cheerfully back to Bucktooth. He wasn't taking *any* direction. Every few minutes, he would glance back at his rider, giving her a contorted toothy grin. His eyes were twinkling. He knew something she didn't.

Mrs. Henry Walker Laroquette was becoming increasingly nervous about this whole California ride-thing. Her derriere rolled side-to-side with disquieting ease. She didn't recall the party pony having quite that action.

Bucktooth half walked, half slid down the sandy trail leading onto Carmel beach proper. Wide-eyed Mrs. L. began to consider that she might lose her battle of the seat, despite a firm grip on the saddle horn and blue tennis shoes properly heel down in the stirrups. Bucktooth repositioned the bit in his mouth and chomped down hard. He leapt the final few feet onto the beach and began a brisk joyful trot. Mrs. L.'s posture, head at 12 o'clock feet at 6PM, immediately shifted to head at 10:30AM, feet at 4PM. Then head at 9:30AM, feet nearing 3.

Bucktooth sensed success and increased the pace to a canter -- galumph galumph-galumph. Mrs. L. grasped that something was seriously amiss and squealed "Oh Help, help, help" in galumph-time.

The panic-high voice couldn't overcome the thrumming of huge hooves on the sand. Sara heard what she thought might be squeals of delight and smiled contentedly at the idea her charges were having a ball.

In an awful turn of events, Mrs. L's tennis shoe took this opportunity to slide completely through the stirrup and wedge her small foot crosswise. Bucktooth did a dancing lurch to avoid a heap of fly-buzzed sea kelp throwing Mrs. L. who, in one acrobatic move, slipped fully sideways to flop against the horse's rhythmically heaving side. Trapped by her foot, she could only hang on hard with double fistfuls of mane and recall with dismay having given up 9:00AM Presbyterian services to go on this ride. Now the Devil's own creature was taking her to her doom!

About that time, Sara realized that something was amiss. It might have been the sight of a rider's foot sticking up in the air near where the saddle horn should have been, and the now bleating peals for help from her charge.

"Stay put! Enjoy the ocean or somethin'!" Sara shouted to the group of now alarmed tourists who had pulled up and were milling around hesitantly.

"Hang on, Ma'am! Help's a-comin'!" Sara yelled, digging heels into Amigo's flanks. Her favorite five-gaited gelding leapt into action, digging flashing hooves into the hard-packed sand sending sparkling white sprays into the morning air. Amigo shot toward Bucktooth like the rock out of King David's slingshot. Sara could see his rider was fully half-mast, head at nine o'clock, one foot somewhere around 5:30 and the other close to 2.

She saw her charge's face staring down at glistening beach flashing just beneath her nose. Life was flashing by in front of her. Just as the two galloping riders reached the massive driftwood log old Bucktooth was intent on leaping, Sara caught the nearest rein, yanked seaward and pulled them all to a galumphing stop. Then Mrs. L's stuck tennis shoe flipped off, popping up into the air, which meant Mrs. L. tumbled head over teakettle onto the beach in an

60

undignified sprawl. The girl and the older woman both trembled, various emotions playing across their faces. Ole Bucktooth blew wind in a personal statement of annoyance at having been thwarted. Mrs. L shook for a good two minutes. Sara did a quickie prayer to St. Jude that she would have at least a small sense of humor and opted for the perky approach as a risk mitigation.

"Boy, talk about an adventure! You sure had a great ride, ma'am. Do you want me to saddle up Bucktooth again? I'll tighten that cinch really good this time. No problems!" Sara's eyes held a plea for mercy.

"No, *thank you*," the lady haughtily responded, grabbing up the errant tennis shoe. "I'll walk back." With occasional sharp-edged comments that only God could hear, Mrs. L. set a smartly brisk pace.

Sara firmly led ole Bucktooth toward the waiting crowd of tourist. After all the excitement, the concensus was to return to the stable for a complimentary western breakfast (Sara's idea which she ended up funding). To lighten the mood while they clip-clopped toward the stable, she kicked into tour director mode regaling her charges with every historical tidbit she could recall. She made sure they sloooowly savored the extraordinary Carmel coastal view, and pointed out places of interest in excruciating detail. It was a mercy that Mrs. Laroquette chose not to sue.

Later that year someone on the Town Council nitpicked the aromatic presence of surf-bobbing road apples noting that they bothered beachcombers (most likely personal guests of the Council member or maybe even Mrs. L!) Sara just had to speak out. At the next council meeting she got the courage to stand tall and opine that such pettiness appeared to be pure-dee anti-horse balderdash since the everyday stink of decaying seaweed far surpassed the nicely organic horse stuff. Her parents, who thought she was at the Bing Crosby Youth Center listening to a local band, were aghast to read all about the daughter's impassioned plea for plain common sense (a phrase which she had impoliticly used) in the morning issue of the Carmel Pine Cone. Papa Henry was so stinky irked that he went for a walk, an unfortunate choice of activity as neighbors then grabbed his elbow, jawboning ad nauseum on Sara's brass and political issues in which he had zero interest.

Having gained sympathy from the horsey community but not the Town Council, Sara and the stable folks had to bite the bit and find another place to take tourists as the entire beach now became off limits. Plan B was a sharp *left* turn onto the lane bordering the grazing pasture, instead of the habitual right toward the beach. The narrow trail wound its way along the dry riverbed, underneath the Route 1 bridge, and up through the artichoke fields to inland meadows of ancient gnarled live oaks soaking up Carmel Valley warmth.

Sara found ample opportunity to retell legends of the "Old Ones, Tribes of the California Coast" whose members tended sacred groves from generation unto generation for hundreds of years. She described coastal shell-traders trekking into the mountains, of great shell mounds hundreds of miles north where the seashells had been pulverized, and where dried fish had been traded for game. She told of scientists discovering ground shells mulched in ten foot deep trenches around the sacred circular groves of giant sequoias, and of fires being purposely set on the tree's uphill side to build up immunity to parasites.

As the tourists wound through the oak groves she pointed out broad white bands around trunks of the oldest live oak trees, and how branches looped strangely earthward before twisting back skyward.

"The branches were trained," she explained, "by tying them with ropes for oh generations and generations. When they're low to the ground like that, gathering acorns for food or trade is a *lot* easier. And that white stuff on the trunks? Bet you think it's paint, don't you. Not paint, nope, not a bit of it! "

She paused for effect then gleefully revealed, "Seashell paste! Probably spread on by the same Old Ones who dragged wicker baskets full of shells up into our northern California groves. The paste not only fed trees minerals but protected them against buggy pesty things, just like the great sequoias". Nodding with deep respect, "The Old Ones were very, *very* wise."

Once in awhile she caught nods, and a particularly deep gaze from another rider. They would share a slow smile of knowing; an understanding that there was much more Ancient Secret wisdom yet to be divulged.

"We know," the shared smiles said, "because we *remember*!" And that made perfect sense to Sara although at the time she couldn't really give a logical justification for the gut sense of rightness.

And the end of most rides, as the last weary charge clopped into the stable yard just downhill from the old Mission Basilica, Sara would slide off Amigo and sigh with satisfaction.

"At last I've found what these bowed legs are good for. They may not be ballet perfect, but they're perfect for wrapping around a good horse!"

But heaven forbid Sara should share such triumphs. Such parental knowledge might lead to expectations of a public performance! That the Gertners demurred taking their daughter anywhere when she reeked of stable, which was most of the time, riding guaranteed continued glorious freedom. But it didn't solve the big problem; the utter necessity of accomplishing something to parade with pride at the annual family reunion. Teaching tourists to ride and thoroughly enjoying oneself outdoors were not, after all, Gertner-approved career options.

An ever willingness to please coupled with pit-bull tenacity finally led to a possible career alternative. There was a way to have a private quiet career *and* achieve the parental seal of approval: Sara revealed to parents, who had actually pretty well figured it out on their own, that she was an omnivorous reader who was leaning toward librarianship. In a pinch, she would even curl up with Papa Henry's leather-bound Autobiography of Ben Franklin, an oversized volume of *New Yorker Magazine* cartoons, or stand in front of open kitchen cabinets organizing cans by size and label color. In a family of academics, reading and attention to precise scientific order were virtues cultivated and lauded. Mattie and Henry also agreed that it was highly unlikely that Sara would be requested to do either before a live audience.

As others outgrew nicknames, or had the problem professionally fixed, Sara was dismayed when "Birdlegs Gertner" stubbornly refused to disappear. That she was the second tallest student in the entire school, overshadowed only by "Leggety Ann" Lipschitz, did not seem reasonable justification for folks doggedly hanging onto the odious nickname. And it wasn't just schoolmates who had become used to "Birdlegs." At the Hawkeyesville reunion, the aunties would only use her given name "Sara Jane Gertner" when speaking directly to her in a firm tone of voice, which generally meant one had been caught making an error in good judgment or bad manners. The rest of the time she was, alas, "La Petite Birdlegs," or "our good ole Birdlegs."

Over afternoon iced-tea, the Hawkeyesville aunties could be overheard chirping good-naturedly, "Did you hear what Birdlegs fell for *this* year? And she is *still* scared about getting warts! Can you imagine that? More tea, Livie dear? "

CHAPTER EIGHT

MOSQUITO SUMMER

The day dawned boding boredom. Along Alder Street, tree shadows sharpened black edges against hot asphalt and the air was honey-thick with humidity. Morning had barely begun and already the boys knew it would be pure-dee miserably hot.

Early morn was best for hunkering down on the old green porch swing, or for kicking it in ever higher arcs that "accidentally" and repeatedly whomped the petals off a trellis-full of golden honeysuckle climbing into the half-moon gutter. Velocity and impact properly timed, neither the gutter nor the trellis would collapse. That was the plan.

Eyeballing up on the backswing, amid a peppering of sticky-sweet pollen, Preston could see there were just enough ten-penny nails still stuck into the porch to keep the trellis up and Dad's voice down.

Early morn was the perfect time to drag boy-scruffy loafers across Grandma's new-painted porch. It was the very best place to contemplate the coming day in a blissful refuge of soggy shade. And it was the bestest most perfect opportunity for applying finishing touches to that Machiavellian, Rube Goldbergian plan concocted the previous Wisconsin winter.

This morning <u>had</u> to be the perfect time and the finishing had to be done fast because every biting black fly in town would soon converge upon the swing -- a phenomenon never fully explained except that the winged evils arrived and departed precisely when the boys did.

An intense need to succeed this particular morning was motivated by it being the very *last* vacation day in Hawkeyesville. Ah, what beatifics Preston and Eldridge had been these past weeks. Not once had they really socked it to Cousin Birdlegs.

"It's a slow death, boredom is," Preston muttered.

Eldridge glanced toward his younger brother and they shared a wicked grin. Recalling the memorized litany forced upon them back in Wisconsin, the boys slowed their trellis-thwacking swing, sat up military-straight, folded hands pristinely in their laps and put on their best imitation of Sabbath-pure faces.

In unison they chanted solemnly:

"Yes, Father, we will abstain from all unkind and thoughtless deeds this summer. We will not do those things which we ought not to do unto dear Cousin Sara. Yes, Father, we would like to have car privileges before we turn thirty. We vow to be proper gentlemen and not bring more shame upon this house. Ahhhhh-*men*!"

But this was hardly the time for detente or worries about being grounded forever. Only this day remained and they couldn't go without at least one primo summer-hot-gotcha memory to roll around in, to savor during their tortuous trek back to the frozen world of academe. Pride was at stake and within moments opportunity would pass utterly by. Subtlety of the devious bent would be required (that would be Eldridge's Congressional-level finesse), a smattering of introductory biology and a scapegoat -- with bird legs. Voila! Ergo sum victorium est -- we are victorious!

Now Iowa during the latter days of August isn't merely hot. Mother Nature kicks the Midwest misery level up to Acutely Thermogenic, oozing limpid vapor-breath tendrils over Hawkeye Eden, pre-wilting salads and sinners alike. Then she adds to the slough-brew a form of swamp life unchanged since the Pleistocene – a beady-eyed bewinged thing that since Spring had dined on stuff environmentalists and even the dog considered unhealthful. Voracious, insatiable, known to carry off small sheep: the Iowa mosquito.

Cousin Sara had erred on the side of innocence with a modest desire to tan before heading back into her California fog. She fluttered long brown eyelashes when she said it, having just discovered that faking naiveté' was superior to appearing bright then proceeding to do  something abysmally dim. It was a definite survival device. So far, only Cousin Preston had noticed the mildly flirtatious coyness right off. Sara's air of vulnerability seemed charming even when he caught her faking it, but exactly why it should be so hormonally appealing was still a mystery.

"There's probably something 'morally wrong' in liking girls anyway," he groaned to himself. "Most everything I like seems to be 'morally wrong' these days. Besides, I'll bet even *thinking* that Cousin Sara's sorta cute is sinful, or illegal, or somethin' even worse ..."

Preston tried to ignore enthusiastic hormones while he and Eldridge focused on final plan details. They were well aware that Sara had been raised in a fogbank in more ways than one, in a land where it rarely warmed above 77° amid winged critters of the rosy-throat hummingbird ilk.

"Ya know,'" Eldridge chuckled with superior glee, "Birdlegs thinks mosquitoes are overgrown fruit flies! She's spent the last three weeks under that world-class ugly hat to protect a delicate complexion and now..." pursing lips in a simpering Clara Bow imitation, "*Now* she wants a tan? Poor thing, perhaps *we* could help?..."

The boys chortled, anticipating their super superior most best 'gotcha' ever.

Just before noon, clad in a properly modest pink hibiscus muumuu, Sara pushed open the kitchen's screechy screen door and headed for Muddy Crik. Down by an olive-brown pond fed by summer sluggish creeks was her secret arbor. A hidden hermitage beyond x-ray vision of older Gertners where one might peruse a forbidden almost-torrid novel and catch a fistful of the last rays of summer.

Sara sighed. Paperback in hand, clutching a bottle of extraordinarily fragrant banana-lanolin-coconut tanning oil (provided courtesy of thoughtful male cousins), she strolled down to meet destiny.

Her older and wiser male cousins, who had scientifically determined during earlier reconnoiters that the Beuller's Pond held the greatest per cubic inch population of starving skeeters in three counties, took the sound of the kitchen screen door slamming shut as their cue to immediately depart for town. Ostensibly headed to retrieve Grandma's mail, it was essential to success (no beatings) that they be "no where near Poughkeepsie at the time."

Sara nestled in utter delight behind the blackberry hedge, her secret niche completely shielded from folks up at the house. Gazing over wind rippled wheat on the far side of the stagnant pool, she sighed again. Privacy -- at last!

Firmly grasping the bottle, Sara dumped galoop-galooping contents, making great slathering sweeps along stork-skinny legs. A sickly-sweet bouquet of banana-lanolin-coconut rose in undulating waves from her frog-belly paleness to waft down-wind, over the pond, bulls-eye dead center into the cloud of swarming skeeters.

Sara didn't have time to peruse even dog-eared page 83 of the torrid romance. Turning as one body, skeeters locked homing radar onto the banana-lanolin-coconut and zoomed along that route to paradise at Mach 9. With a heavy thrumming hum, they then shifted into serious overdrive. At the same instant she had rolled to reach for *Lady Pirate Passions*, the cloud blanketed her frog-belliness with zebra stripes that bit. The feasting had begun.

   Blocks and blocks away, Cousins Preston and Eldridge had just cut through Elmer Schroeder's back yard toward the town's central park, a splendid oasis of towering elms, ranks as yet unthinned by a double-whammy of Dutch elm plague and vicious thunderstorms which later rendered 86% into garden mulch. Such remnants of the First Forest, smack dab in the middle of many Midwestern towns, were civilized places for staging family picnics, strolling after church, and for town fairs of the old-fashioned no-neon kind with prizes for pickle-loaf and exhibits of hulking antique iron-wheeled steam-driven farm machinery. Uncle Henry had explained the curious rural sign "No Lugs on Roadway" which the boys presumed referred to idiot drivers.

   "Au contraire," Uncle Henry slowly explained so they'd savor the story appropriately. "Lugs are those monstrous earth-grabbing spikes adorning the flat-steel wheels of ancient tractors long since gone to rust. Local legends speak of these beasts materializing from pearly-pale swirling mists when an autumn moon is truly full, their ghostly lumbering progress echoing, echoing across dimly distant fields...beware, beware the spikes!" Then he would say "BOO!" really loud and cause Preston to have to change his underwear.

   Ambling along the time-worn path through Hawkeyesville Park, the boys reached an area usually ringing with high-pitched giggles and howls of glee. Preston recalled getting the hiccups a lot after they'd played there. It was the designated Kiddies' Zone replete with twenty-foot high swings and a faded rainbow-patterned circular platform canted at a 15 ° angle with tubular pipe hand-rails radiating from its hub. The Genuine Patented Tilt & Spin was guaranteed to make little kids throw up if spun around fast enough. That is, if they didn't first skid off, become airborne and tumble into the grass some distance away. Off by itself was a long series of heavy duty teeter-totters which looked to have been barn siding in an earlier incarnation. It was Eldridge who discovered early on that leaping off his end at the proper moment would cause Preston at the other end to slam into the earth with a dust-raising wallop, after which he would stutter or have hiccups for a good hour. He was amazed that Preston was dumb enough to get on the totters time after time, knowing what was likely to happen. He figured eventually Pres would wise up. Pres figured every year was the one Eldridge would stop bailing out early. Both boys were stubborn. The hiccups went on for years.

As they continued cutting across the grass, carefully avoiding proper paths, the boys grinned at the memory of an enormous Brahma bull whose thoughts turned to love on that very spot during last year's Town Fair. The massive bundle of love loosed itself and proceeded to pay ardent court to several of Mr. Diedermeier's prize Holstein cows. The dewey-eyed creatures were apparently unimpressed. They continued grazing sweet grass around the gleaming bronze water fountain, not even glancing around for a "how-de do and who-are-you?"

Diedermeier spoke of dining on Brahma prairie oysters in the immediate near future which made no sense to the boys, oysters not being an Iowa crop and all. The speed with which Mamas spun children to face the pink and white Gothic-spired Lutheran church, pointed out activities of distant grey squirrels, or firmly pressed goggle-eyed faces to heaving bosoms, was truly amazing. Preston and Eldridge had thought such behavior a tad odd, these being farm kids after all whose daily chores were intimately involved with nature of Mother Nature.

They had come to U.S. Route 61 which bisected the town and ran parallel to the railroad tracks. Dashing across the two-lane concrete highway, looking both ways, was getting risky. Traffic was up to the heady rate of one vehicle every ten minutes! The duo then rounded 5th Street, walking on the outside of the sidewalk as they passed a particular grey granite 19th century building with a huge pair of intricately carved wooden doors and a colossal string of beads hanging on the bronze doorknob.

St. Margaret of the Heartland, with its mysterious incense, painted statues and real wine (not Welch's grape juice) was a taboo

71

place. They didn't really know why, but Aunt Livie had gone on at
length about visiting St M.'s being immediately followed by lightning
bolts for some theological difference of opinion the boys were quite
unable to fathom. She also mentioned something about Father
O'Reilly who loved coming to dinner to discuss a whole-family
conversion which apparently scared the pants off Lutheran-tithing
Gertners. Uncertain as to whether God was Roman Catholic,
German Lutheran, or maybe even wore a really neat eagle-feathered
war bonnet, or saffron robes like *National Geographic* Hindus and
Buddhists, they opted to avoid finding out fer sure and bein' fried to
a heathen crisp in the process.

Rounding the final corner, on which stood the equally taboo
pool hall, the boys sauntered down the only commercial street in
Hawkeyesville, little changed since the booming 1890's. Parking
meters were conspicuously absent. Farm trucks and station wagons
angled neatly in diagonal or parallel parking slots along the two
blocks of asphalt-patched concrete. At the fire house, the noon
whistle went off with a horrific blast and the boy's automatic
thought was to Duck-and-Cover.

Old Doc Palmer, who just happened to be strolling past the
alley, stopped to stare at two squatting forms in dungarees huddled

against the thick brick wall of the old pharmacy. Over thin wire-rimmed glasses, he stared at the queer creatures whose arms were clenched protectively over bowed heads. He loudly cleared his throat. Eldridge lifted one elbow and peeked up from under it.

"You're young George's boys, aren't you?" Doc queried politely. "Don't you have noon whistles where you come from?"

Sheepishly the boys unwound from their graceless squats, rose to casually dust khaki pants, finger-comb their hair, and head to the sidewalk.

"Sure, Dr. Palmer. 'Course we do. Nice day, isn't it, sir? Doesn't look like rain yet. Well, we have to be getting the mail now. Goodbye, sir."

Striding with great official purpose toward the Post Office, Preston stared straight, fists jammed into his pants pockets. When he thought the Doc had had time to enter the General Store, as was his habit, Preston hung his head in despair and muttered over and over and over, "Criminey, what dorks we musta looked like. Dorks! Oh, criminey..."

Just ahead, down on the left side of Main Street, stood the neat brown brick single-story Post Office, efficiently managed by Widow Kruzbacher since at least the time George Washington was a boy. Within its cool dimly lit recesses, the dull-gleam of hundreds of bronze twin-dial postal boxes could be made out, rising splendidly along two full walls. The boys had each been given the proper setting for one dial, so it would take both to unravel the mysterious alpha-numeric combination and retrieve accumulated mail, most simply marked "Mrs. G., Alder Street, City."

After passing the obligatory six minutes in out-of-state Wisconsin gossip with the Widow K. who didn't travel much these days, they made a beeline toward the tall screened door directly across the street, the door that announced in a piercing rusty screech one's entry into the wondrous land of Wilson's Creamery & Soda Fountain. Being momentarily the possessors of the stupendous sum of fifty cents apiece, Preston and Eldridge proceeded to squander the entirety of their fortune on supper-killing root beer floats, savoring creamery-fresh vanilla ice cream as it melted down long-handled spoons and slid down long hungry gullets. By now, nearly an hour had been dutifully frittered away. Eyes glittering in anticipation, the boys agreed it was time to behold what the skeeters hath wrought.

By the time scruffy shoes clomped back across the front porch, it was all over but the clamoring of Mama Mattie and the Aunts -- vigorously daubing potions upon mottled, blotched, bumpy as a summer squash Sara. Perched atop the traditional tall kitchen stool, submitting with severely bent dignity to application of at least three gazillion stinky green-tinted calamine polka dots, she was glaring daggers in their direction. At least they thought she was glaring.

"Hard to tell, ya know," Eldridge whispered from behind his hand, "Little eyeballs all swollen squinty like that."

The boys might well have survived with only a stern lecture had not Preston been unable to resist sniggering.

"Gee Sara Jane, you look kinda like a pickle on a stick..." To his amazement, his genteel cousin launched from the top rung of the stool in an athletic arc, fingers extended toward his throat.

"Gonna kill you, you **rat!**" was followed by a lightning fast belly tackle which morphed into a tumbling thrashing ball of legs and arms, rolling into the dining room and under a table neatly set for family supper. The appallingly unlikely sight was vividly engraved in memories of this event. Also the sight of dinner plates, silverware and a large bowl of lima beans bouncing into the air like popcorn off a hot woodstove.

In bruised and mottled splendor, they stood nose-to-wallpaper in opposite corners of the living room. Gertners arriving for supper, who'd missed seeing the really big show personally, could only gasp and head back to the front porch to hear the tale from Aunt Livie holding court on the swing. Aunt Livie *always* got the story right.

Gertner ladies clucked, "Such language! My, what a perfectly dreadful display. Yes, yes the bruises will eventually fade. They do, you know. And Miss Sara's bumps should be gone by the end of next week. When did you say her classes begin, Mattie dear? Oh fudge! *Next* Monday?"

Birdleg's did *what?* No Foolin'!

Form
color:

For public retelling, family agreed to use the Revised Standard Version since the original was unthinkably un-Gertnerlike, and certainly indescribable --with a straight face.

CHAPTER NINE

Homestead Summer

Summer in Hawkeyesville was not complete without at least one evening in Grandma's parlor where curious cousins were crammed full of clan legends and yarns about life on the 1850's homestead. That there were tales rather than visits was entirely due to Uncle Herman.

The very idea of trying to keep an eye on four energetic nosy city kids -- any child from a burg larger than Hawkeyesville was a "city kid" -- would send him out to the front porch rocker where he'd stay until fireflies nested in his hair.

Aunt Gert was sure and certain there was another reason for Herman's unwillingness to have youthful visitors. Grudgingly, she divulged grim reality to Aunts Livie, Minerva and Mama Mattie during a potato peeling session at Grandma Gertner's. Definitely the coolest place to be on an Iowa August afternoon, the tin-ceilinged kitchen was their sanctuary. It was also where their systematic assessment of male Gertner quirkiness made tasks go ever so much faster.

"Well, it's like this," Aunt Gert divulged, as another curling peel plopped neatly into the blue crockery bowl.

"As you know, like most Gertner men my Herman has his set ways of doing things. He's most methodical, Herman is. Well," Gert nervously wiped her flushed face with a rainbow-striped kitchen towel, "Herman has...well he has a bad case of *radios.* " She paused, spud peels plopping a tad bit faster. After a full minute of silence, Aunt Livie shot up her hand mid-peel, signaling for attention.

She turned and stared directly at Gert's bowed head. No response. Gert kept whipping long russet ribbons of tater peel into the sky blue bowl. Livie then queried, with the slightest edge of annoyance to her voice, "*And...* Gert? Most of us have radios these days. Most of us had radios in 'those days' too, even if they *were* parlour pieces big as a china cabinet. So what's so special about our Herman's?"

Aunt Gert was awkward and uncomfortable. Carefully laying down the peeling knife, she began repeatedly smoothing the apron with her fingertips. With a rush the confession tumbled out.

"Herman doesn't have just *one* radio, my dears. He has at least fifteen or *twenty.* I mean, there are at least *five* in every room of the house, the outhouse excepting of course, and each is tuned to a particular station. It's worth your life to fiddle with one of his precious radios and heaven forbid you should move the dial the teensiest bit even if all you just want to hear is 'The Rest of the Story!'"

"Mercy! There, I've <u>said</u> it. That's why he can't abide the notion of another batch of children out on the place, ours-are-grown-and-gone-thank-God. Hermie knows that sure as sin one of them will get into their heads a need to fiddle with the sacred radios and instead of 4:48AM weather or 6:06AM hog prices, he's going to get an earful of that dreadful rappity rock and roll!"

Now looking utterly relieved, having dropped an impressive emotional load, Gert began quartering peeled potatoes for her Second Place Gertnerized Sweet Pickle German Salad.

"Excuse me, dear." It was Aunt Livie again, who insisted on one getting right to the point without needless digressions or dawdling.

"Why in heaven's name does he do that?! Surely one radio would do quite nicely. Perhaps even two, at the utmost. I mean, it's hardly thrifty to indulge oneself with 'fifteen or twenty' when waaay fewer would quite do."

"One would think so, wouldn't one?" Aunt Gert nodded. "But you see Herman has each tuned to a particular station, as I said. One for weather, one bellies, and one set for local and regional news but frankly I can never remember which that is. Being a Gertner man, he claims it's practical and therefore it has become the absolute only and best way. *He* always knows where to go and which contraption will have the afternoon church news." It was obvious from her skinny-lipped expression that she did not share such technical directional expertise.

"Could be worse, I've no doubt. Plenty worse sins that having too many radios in the house..." Pencil-thin lips belied the generosity of her words. The sound of a particularly large potato thudding into the mixing bowl put an explanation point on the end of her statement.

The ladies nodded in solemn unison, then heaved a collective sigh. Each could recall plenty worse sins right off the bat, mostly having to do with idiosyncrasies in their respective Gertner men.

Later that evening, after the good china had been hand-dried and put away, Gertner ladies had "little girl chats" with their respective Gertner men. Men-folk in turn cornered Uncle Herman when his head was in the fridge looking for more pie. They herded him down the short stairs to the back porch screen door and out toward Grandma's medicinal herb garden for a "little man-chat" of their own. An hour later, a grumpalous Uncle Herman clumped into the parlor, fists shoved deep into pants pockets, with the grudging announcement that the cousins would be given their first taste of real homestead farm life the very following day. Grandma and the aunties smiled tight little smiles of victory and graciously nodded to Herman. Herman wheeled around, clumped out to the front porch and hunkered glumly on the swing until fireflies nested in his hair. He didn't even want his normal after-dinner beer. Too down in the dumps. Too miserable. Too grumpalous. The swing banged against the trellis.

Come early morning, an ecstasy of cousins piled into Uncle George's Ford station wagon primed with visions of undulating cornfields, standard issue text-book farm critters, plus a stern finger-waving admonition from Aunt Livie.

'Listen up, you young people! Uncle Herman's grandfather Otis, now that would be your great-grandfather on your paternal side, fell nose first right down to the bottom of the well during construction and although he didn't break anything falling, he did quite promptly die from an invisible noxious gas. And the hired man, now let me see -- that would have been Carstens Lars Schroeder, Senior -- well he nearly died trying to fish out the sad remains, so for heaven's sake, children, stay *away* from that well!"

Cousins Preston, Eldridge, and Roswell exchanged quick glances of undisguised glee. First stop - the well!

Now, the Gertner family homestead was a good distance beyond Hawkeyesville out on the old two-lane county road north of Davenport. Indeed, it was forty minutes (if one's luck held) spent threading a maze of unmarked (and occasionally unmapped) dirt farm roads meant more for horses and tractors than modern cars. The wry philosophy of Iowa rural signage was: "If you don't know where you're going, and haven't directions from folks at the other end, then you haven't any business going there." This was a personal trial for Uncle George who hadn't been out to the home place in nearly twenty years and had to rely on spotty memory. It would have been in poor taste to ask Herman for directions, especially after those persuasively detailed boyhood reminiscences out by the medicinal garden.

George knew that *eventually* he would spot familiar gently sloping hillsides lush with alfalfa, corn, or fallow pasture, depending on year and season, and that there at the base of Petersen's Knob would be a simple two-storied white clapboard farmhouse built for practical shelter rather than architectural splendor. The architectural gem of any farm was, of course, the barn. Barns were painstakingly crafted and artfully adorned. After all, they protected expensive livestock, feed, seed, farm implements, and the occasional inherited black horse-hair sofa. A house was just for Lutherans working out karma by pouring money into the black loam. It wouldn't do to be fancy.

"To find the house, just follow the fields." Uncle George intoned to the captive cousins in the Ford. "Where the crops aren't, cows are. Where the cows aren't, pigs are. And in the little space where none of the above are, there you'll find Uncle Herman and Aunt Gert."

That last bit raised cousinly concern, expressed in a whisper by Roswell. "I'm not sure Aunt Gert would like bein' where even piggies won't go..."

Uncle Herman's turned out to be a place of true marvels, the finest of which (Cousins Preston, Eldridge and Roswell later agreed) was a first-class gaggle of geese scattered across the side yard. Yowzah, Buck Rogers!

Piling out of the dusty Ford, cousins were straight away lined up on the front porch by Uncle Herman and presented with **The Homestead Rules**, all three barrels of which appeared aimed specifically at the boys.

- No running through the corn. You'll slice yourselves to ribbons.
- No doing " number 1" in the creek unless it's well downstream to the Holsteins and the house.
- No touching any radio anywhere, ever, period, end of story. And I mean it!

Aunt Gert passed around oven-warm chocolate chip cookies, sun-warm peaches from the side yard, and nodded toward a wicker basket of lurking omnipresent prunes just in case someone had a real yen. Uncle Herman relaxed some and began pointing out first the nearby cow barn, the big machinery and storage barn across the road, an ancient slant-roofed much-patched poultry house, then moved beyond to "back-80" field boundaries (that would be the eighty acres out back of the house). Getting up a head of steam, Herman continued describing all the various criks and larger stream feeds to the river, finishing up with the exact whereabouts of an extraordinary limestone cave guaranteed to be infested with brown bats. Empowered and emboldened with knowledge of the home place's true geography, the cousins were released into the wild to roam whilst grown-ups retired to blissful kitchen coolness for home-brewed cinnamon iced-tea.

Scooting around the house and scouting out the infamous well, the boys were truly dismayed to find an immovable grey concrete slab with a silver painted hand pump planted firmly dead center.

"Well, fudgebuttsit!" muttered Roswell, kicking at a dirt clod. "Guess we'll never know what those 'noxious gases' smelled like, huh guys?" Roswell had yet to properly master Mama Mattie's "fussbudget" epithet of dismay.

Eldridge glowered with superiority upon his much younger cousin. "Roswell Bettendorf Gertner, can't you think about anything but stuff that stinks? Jeez Louise, there's plenty other cool stuff around here -- like *Injun* stuff. "Turning to Preston he confided, Uncle Herman said he found piles of arrowheads out in the back forty once, down by Willow Crik. Wanna bet we can find tomahawks? And maybe some great big scalping axes, too? C'mon!"

Preston pulled a torn slip of yellow-lined note-paper from his dungarees. "Wait a minute. Aunt Gert wrote down the names of the First People. That's what she calls Injuns. She says Injuns isn't nice and we shouldn't say it." He squinted at the penciled script, then read his notes:

"1. Illinois tribes of Algonquin-Ritwan

2. Iowa tribes of the Prairie Sigh-oh-oxs"

"That's 'Soo,' Pres. You really gotta try harder, ya know. I heard Mom tellin' Dad that she's sure you're gonna big-time not make the grade in American History...and you know what *that* means." Preston's face paled beneath his freckled tan. He was slightly sick to his stomach.

"Yeah..." he groaned. "It means six weeks of summer school with old Miz Weeblefonger." The thought alone made him break out in goose bumps and chicken skin.

Turning to Roswell, Eldridge lit up with sudden enthusiasm. "But wait a minute, *now* we know what to look for. It's gotta have 'Illinois Algonquin' or 'Iowa Sioux' on it somewhere, right? Like "Made in Japan" stuff at Murphy's Five & Dime. That makes it easy!

We'll all be rich and on the news! Yowzah, last one to the Knob eats fat gooshy worms!"

Filled with visions of grisly wonders, and a properly motivational educational grounding, the terrible trio raced along the fence line cow path. Their distant landmark: a particular grove of ancient willows at the foot of Petersen's Knob overlooked by the alluring bat cave. Twas a *National Geographic* scientific all-male expedition bound to consume a goodly chunk of the afternoon. Back at the farm house, older Gertners sighed with relief. At least four hours of boy-less peace was near at hand. They clinked glasses of iced-tea in sweet thanksgiving.

"God bless us, every one" prayed Aunt Gert.

Sara, who had at long last given up trying to be one of the boys, watched from the front porch as the dust cloud and shouts of camaraderie faded into the distance. It was bitter-sweet, especially for a tomboy at heart, but she was supposed to be a proper young lady now and such disappointments were bound to happen. She lifted her chin and scanned the horizon for properly self-improving activities to occupy the long summer afternoon.

Across the heat-shimmered asphalt Sara briskly marched intent on her target of first choice. Just beyond the low-slung chicken house was the main barn. It appeared eternally old, maybe even as old as great-*great* grandfather! She walked along the path toward the doorway, looking intently at details of the barn's construction and was surprised to see crumbled chunks of creamy foundation limestone split into the weeds. The fact that they were in the weeds and not beneath the barn did not appear to matter to the barn, having been solidly and properly Gertnered from the get go. That meant engineered to last!

Blacksmith-forged hinges fastened weathered dutch-doors with thick square-head nails. Glancing down the long side of the barn facing south-bound traffic she got a closer look at the gigantic painted Red-Man chewing tobacco advert. Even heavily weathered with gaps in the picture where broken boards had been replaced, the

"Fine Chew" handsome Chief was heart-stoppingly inspiring. Sara had never seen anything like it in Carmel. Inspired, she pondered, "How would Papa Henry and the neighbors feel about my painting a mural of wild-eyed ponies galloping down the beach. I could put it right there on the big street-side of our garage." Humm. That had distinct possibilities.

She had reached the dutch-doors again and yanked the knotted cord latch string. With a rust-grinding creak, the door swung open to let her pass. Eyes adjusting to the interior gloom, Sara walked face-first into a country-sized spider web and could have sworn Miss Spider grinned as if the girl might possibly prove tasty.

"Aaagh! Ugh! Yuckers!" She grabbed a hoe and batted down the creepy web, banging the tool against the barndoor at the end of her "batter-up" swing. Then Sara took her first tentative steps into a real live farm barn, a place filled with Iowa history's mysteries.

She stared with awe at massive adze-hewn beams overhead. Those irregular hatch marks could even have come from that rusty hand-adze poking up from its dust blanket beneath the window-ledge. Sparrows flashed toward invisible nests in the rafters; crickets chatted amongst themselves in leg-rubbing cricket-code.

Closing her eyes, she inhaled aromas unlike anything at the salt-aired beach or her touristy stable. Sun-warmed barn-wood centuries old. Faint scents of animalness emanating from blackened mule harness hanging over a long empty stall. Spills of gasoline, tractors oozing lubricating oil, decades of dust, generations of milk cows and strolling chickens. She slowly opened her eyes, savoring the smells, and whispered "Boy, it sure doesn't smell like Safeway..."

And what was that? Past the spoke-wheeled wagon with peeling green paint? It appeared to be a vertical line, a support column tree-trunk thick that soared into the gloom toward second floor rafters. It was held together by wooden pegs as fat as a man's finger. "Could those things have come from the First Forest?" she wondered in awe. If they did, they were bound to have magical powers. That's what her Camp Fire Girl counselor had said. *Magical...*

Displayed on a greyed board over Uncle George's main workbench was an array of tools and strange-looking devices whose peculiar uses she could only wildly guess. There were things with multiple springy hinges, things with moon-shaped arcs of teeth, heavy-weight hand carved pulleys with age-brittled leather belts, draft horse trace chains, vicious-looking hay bale hooks, and an extensive collection of ornately-cast iron tractor seats. Beneath the bench, leaning against the faded blue winter kerosene stove, was a woven fruit basket that had seen much better days. With bottom strips busted-out, it was currently home to the latest batch of semi-feral kittens which would one day be barn cats. Sara had strict orders to not to go near them as Moochy, their vermin-eating mama, had been known to launch claws-first full-rototill on all comers except kindly Uncle George.

"*And*, they are not very sanitary." Aunt Gert advised, one eyebrow meaningfully raised.

Proper investigation of a farm barn takes time, but time became irrelevant once Sara become engrossed in treasures discovered one after another. It was her very own archeological dig, just like she read about during the Egyptian phase at the library. She longed for a sketchpad and was annoyed that she had taken off without a proper notebook. Still she couldn't waste time going back to the house for such tools. She might miss something critical and fabulously wonderful!.

Toward the back, on the side that was less barn-like and more finished storage rooms, she spied a distant stairway. There was something odd about it, Sara thought. She walked slowly, examining each emerging detail with scientific care. What was it that made this simple old barn stair seem so strange, so extraordinary? Finally coming within a few feet, she gasped in astonished wonder. What had caught her eye as "out of place for a barn" was an amazing grace of carved handrail spanning the angle of space with gentle strength. Stair treads appeared to lift lightly, to soar toward the rafters and to her eyes trying to adjust to the shadows, they had a subtle – glow. Not only that, but the handrail was carved from a single tree!

Closing her eyes, she ran caressing fingertips over the natural limb's silken-worn surface. In a dizzying moment, she sensed all the hands that had touched that handrail before her, as though they were her own hands. In her minds eye there arose a dreamlike montage of faces: brawny, heavily bearded men; a laughter of scampering flaxen-haired children; women of square-jawed strength, thick braided coils of hair forming a halo, a crown upon their heads. Sara could hear the rustling of long black skirts hiked up one-handed as their wearer ascended to the stairway.

Behind her eyes, Sara watched feeling outside of time and space as the hand on the railing changed shape and size and color; was youthful, masculine, womanly, then fragilely frail with delicate spots from age.

Sara felt dizzy. Her head whirled and she had a hard time wanting to return from wherever she was. She staggered back and shook her head a little to clear away the whirling mental pictures. When her eyes opened, now more accustomed to the dimness of the barn, she stared directly and clearly at the staircase. She was stunned. The beautiful flight didn't lead to anywhere in the barn. In fact, it leaned against the barn wall disconnected from anything but its own memories. It almost felt holy. This was a part of the homestead that no one, not even Aunt Livie, had shared with the cousins.

There was a for-real mystery in all this but Sara told herself to be patient. She would have to wait for that special private moment with Mama, when she was rested and in a good mood, to ask what *really* just happened. Practical Hawkeyesville Gertners didn't own up to having mystical experiences, or to there being spiritually active real estate between heaven and earth. But Mama's Baton Rouge family, on the other hand, spent an inordinate amount of time dancing amongst the threads that held the worlds apart.

That having been said, Sara knew that there had to be a for-real way to get to the floor above. Around a short wall, to the right of the stairway to nowhere, she spotted it; a wooden staircase ladder which extended to a large trap-door in the ceiling. Although it didn't have the memories that the magic staircase had, it was a marvel in and of itself. Each step on the ladder seemed carved of a different type of wood, or so it appeared what with wear and age and all. And the upright spindles that attached to the sturdy plain handrail were – ohmygosh! –a whittled tree branch fit into individually augured holes.

Sara gathered up her courage and with a firm grip began to climb up to the dark trap-door in the wide-planked ceiling. A long metal cable ran to a system of sash weights and pulleys, like an old fashioned window but without the smashed fingers. It was surprisingly easy to manage. As it slid open, she sensed strangely unfamiliar shapes in dust-shrouded shadows. An afternoon sun overtopped the barn, its rays slicing into the gloom, bit by bit carving away darkness. Its revelations tempted the imagination, lured her toward the deliciously mysterious unknown. What a magnificent adventure!

The room was considerably larger than she'd imagined it would be. Neatly stacked against the wall of a central hall was a bank of sturdy iron-bound steamer trunks. *And* they were unlocked! There seemed to be three or four smaller rooms which opened onto the hallway. In the first was an accumulation of old furniture; sideboards, a small white Hoosier kitchen cabinet, small occasional tables with nearly black spindled legs. Over against the south wall Sara spied a sweet little enamel-topped kitchen table piled with circular hat boxes inscribed with names of shops long since gone for office parks. What about that oval lavender box elegantly inscribed:

"Miss Amelia's Millinery, Muscatine Iowa"

It looked older than Great-Grandma! If she opened it, would Aunt Gert's knack for knowing when someone was "doing what they ought not to" send her dashing pell-mell across the road to

87

protect this stuff from prying eyes? Sara felt courageous, and besides she was being very very quiet.

There were wooden fruit crates containing lithographed tins, old medicine flasks, remnants of dress goods. In the second room, Sara discovered a ghostly sheet-draped dress form standing watch against those who oughtn't be there. She could just barely see an old-fashioned floor-length dress with tatted lace and sharp pleats. Everywhere were visual riches and delights.

Did she dare pry open that trunk lid in the hall, even a tiny bit? Then her scientific Gertner training kicked in. Before one tore into something unknown, one was always to observe and justify ones actions. Deciding for once to observe before rushing headlong into trouble, Sara tugged a dark oak pressed back chair into the center of the room. Sitting gingerly on the edge of its crackling cane seat, she scanned slowly around the room, taking it all in.

The afternoon sun sent shafts of August-bright light shooting through the dust-hazed windows. Golden dust motes flowed in eddies, gliding along shimmering sunbeam rivers of afternoon warmth. Orange and green print curtains from the 1930's hung dirt-stiff, framing four radiant panes of old rippledy glass. Sara held back an instinctive Virgo urge to polish that glass till it sparkled like a prismic jewel.

"The boys have no idea what great stuff they are missing. There's really ancient history right here in the barn. Maybe old as the Roman Empire!" she mused, staring at an old Latin grammar book.

The workings of the male mind were a mystery to Sara. Pondering the puzzle, she had but recently come to the only logical conclusion: boys, even Cousins Preston and Eldridge whom she held in nearly reverent esteem, had been wired wrong at the factory.

The hours lost their distinctive edges, flowing seamlessly as Sara rummaged and explored, careful to return things to where and how she had found them. At one point she took a break, wondering just what the boys were up to. Wondering about the boys, and what they thought was fun led to more thoughts about the peculiar hard-wiring brain difference between girls and boys. It didn't seem clear cut at all. Not at all scientific. It was just another confusing growing up challenge from the Factory that was way beyond her young girl understanding.

"Everybody's a child of God, my dear" Mama Mattie had advised. "Regardless of how they dress or the color lipstick they choose, it's none of our business to judge or decide. It's our job just to love and be loved. I think that's pretty much the nut of it all." That was the only sermon Mama gave on the subject, and so it *must* have been the definitive answer. Mama was very wise. Mama had also opined that there were no ugly people, just some folks had more character in their faces than others. Sara let it go for another wiser day. She still thought Mrs. Weeblefonger had waaay more character than most.

Sara gingerly made her way back down the ladder, staring straight on at fastenings of every rung lest a desperate fear of heights kick in and lock her permanently halfway down. "One step. One step. One step." She talked to herself, taking one step at a time. Hopping off the bottom step with a heartfelt sigh of relief, she leaned over and briskly tousled curls which *had* to be plumb full of cobwebs and barn dirt. All of a sudden, she had a serious case of nose itch, instantly followed by a barn-rattling "Aaah-*CHOOOEY!* Agh!"

Extracting the tail of a perky ironed-that-morning blouse from pink plaid pedal-pushers, Sara vigorously rubbed her noise maker then neatly retucked the shirt. The clean spot smack in the middle of a dirt-smudged face made her freckled nose stand out like a beacon. Blissfully unaware, she walked toward to the barn door and gazed beyond. The doorway framed a view vastly different from her familiar west coast haunts.

"That silo over there looks like a rocket aimed at the stars..." she whispered. She had always wanted to take a romantic rocket ship into the stars.

"And see how sunlight through the corncrib makes checkered shadows by the chicken coop?" Sara decided that she liked the homestead even if there *weren't* any riding horses. As an aside before she started out for the barn, Uncle Herman had made it perfectly clear in no uncertain terms.

"No riding the dairy cows or they'll be giving up cottage cheese instead of milk for your morning cereal. End of discussion." Roger that, over and out.

As her hazel eyes took in dusky cornfields rolling hills into the distance, fading from light emerald to richer shades of lavender as they met the woods, her imagination soared.

"Those hills way over there look like rumbled cloud blankets thrown down from the sky." She relaxed and let her imagination loose in the paint box of words, crafting more and more precise prose paintings. Then she recalled that piece written for English class which had come to her in the middle of the night. Her teacher seemed particularly pleased even though it *was* supposed to be about the weather.

"As the weeks passed by, Mother Nature exchanged luminous emerald summer frocks for autumn's scarlet-gilt finery. Then too soon came the Turning of the Year and the great cape of ermine and raven's wing. Wrapped warm, she trailed swirling eddies of snow mist in the air as she passed by."

She would remember the farm scene just beyond the barn door threshold and write about it later in her journal. Taking a deep breath, she imprinted the scene into memory. Now, way back in early childhood, so far back that she couldn't exactly remember when she'd started doing it, Sara had made a discovery. It was a remembering technique, actually. If one stared at a particular scene which one really wanted to remember later, if one stared really hard, memorized every detail, then smelled something which was part of that scene, why it could be recalled any time in the future without losing anything of the original! And she found that it helped to also attach a color to the memory, like a gemstone, to make it easier. If she couldn't recall the smell, then at least the color would stick. At least that is how it was supposed to work. And most of the time, Sara observed, it did.

She closed her eyes in a tight squint and took a deep deep breath. The homestead was sharp tang of green tourmaline alfalfa, a dusky warmth of topaz hay, the faded garnet of barn paint, opalescent sour-sweetness of cows just milked, and... Hold it! Something else was wafting on the humid Iowa breeze.

"What's this?" Sara turned slowly one way then another, homing in on the source of sweet non-barn smells. Ahhh, there! That's where it's coming from." Opening her eyes a little, she caught a glint of sunlight on shining tin. Across the road, on top of the little card table on Aunt Gert's front porch...

"There it is!" Eyes closed in utter ultimate bliss. It was the aroma of the celestial spheres. The nose-rose of nirvana. It was —

"Aunt Gert's Dutch apple pie—fresh out of the oven. Oh, wowsers!" Her nose led and the feet quickly followed, zipping across the road and up the steps toward apple-joy.

It was heading into late afternoon. The sun had long since crossed the yardarm and the pirates aboard the good ship Gertner had headed for port. Cousins Preston, Eldridge, and Roswell had raised their virtual cutlasses, hacked and thwacked their way across fields and gullies and imaginary seas until everything ached—and without success. Not one Sioux or Ripawan artifact. They did find a stash of whiskey bottles in a clearing which they suspected were from the local high school neer-do-well boys. Like the ones who hung out in front of the pool hall on Hawkeyesville Main Street. Not one tomahawk was to be found.

But they did find the limestone cave, discovering first hand what was on the floor of bat caves, and they'd had quite an adventure dodging and barely outrunning angry residents of a wasp nest which had somehow become dislodged from its low-hanging maple branch. The good ship Gertner had slid into port and thrown out the anchor just about the time Sara had finished her barn rummage.

Side by side by side, the terrible trio perched along the edge of the home place front porch, rhythmically banging heels against a trembling wooden lattice. The green painted screening nailed around three sides of the porch was to keep pests out, Uncle Herman had said.

"And that includes you boys! I keep *snakes* under there, you know. And black-striped farm snakes are real mean! Last summer one caught a stray nanny goat and swallowed it up clean. Started at a little back hoof and worked its way right on up to the ears. Yep, it did. Then it slithered back under the porch to wait for *dinner!"* Eldridge in particular would recall this tale with horror.

Continued rhythmic thumping of six sturdy heels brought Aunt Gert to the parlour window. Lifting aside frost-white lace curtains, she peered out. The drummers were slumped over, snagging slivers of wood along the edge of her porch and pulling—a contest to see just who could strip out the longest piece of her porch.

"They're getting bored, Herman." She sighed as the curtain folds silently fell back into place. "And that little sneak Roswell is getting cranky to boot. He's starting to screw up his face and whine. You'd better keep an eye on them until their folks are ready to head back." As she walked toward the kitchen, Herman just caught the familiar whispered litany…"Good-thing-ours-are-grown-and-gone, *thank-God…"*

Cousin Preston glanced over at his brother, then elbowed him smartly in the ribs.

"Hey! Eldridge! I'm getting a real bad case of MTBL. What do you think we oughta do about that?"

Cousin Eldridge rubbed his side and glared. "You better cut that out, Pres! No reason you should be getting that MTBL stuff already. And I'm not going to do *anything* about it. When you get bored these days, I always get in trouble!"

MTBL was the boys' secret password. It stood for 'Maximum Tolerable Boredom Level" and its utterance was generally followed by a diligent search for truly elegant insidious amusement.

A raucous honking drifted their way on the warm afternoon breeze. 'Wa-ooonk. Waa-ooonk" the sound waddled with sedate dignity into their line of sight. It was Abigail, the Gertner's watch-goose. Trailing behind her came the latest gaggle of goslings, now fully fledged and full of racket. Bringing up the rear was the great communicator himself -- Martin, the hulking gander. With an

unaccustomed bit of wry humor, Herman had named the pair for
the 8th President and his wife, Martin and Abigail Van Buren.

From the opposite direction, returning from the barn utterly
focused and seemingly oblivious to the world outside of pie, came
their answer to MTBL.

"Boy oh boy," Preston muttered nearly salivating with
delight. "It's Cousin Birdlegs..." Drumming their heels, the Wisconsin
duo glanced at each other and in unison grinned big.

"You thinking what I'm thinking?" Eldridge breathed in
Preston's direction.

"Close enough to get your drift." Preston muttered in return,
trying not to move his lips. "If you've got a plan, you better get it
goin' before Sara gets to the pie." The boys smirked. Relief *was* at
hand!

Roswell stared at his cousins in bald-faced disbelief. "You
guys aren't gonna do what I think you're gonna do...*are* you?"

Eldridge gave Roswell a quick nudge. "Could be... Watch
and learn from the masters!" With straight solemn faces, which they
knew was the only surefire way to approach their prey, the two
older boys hopped off the porch and sauntered real casual-like
toward Sara.

"Hey there, Cuz. Guess what? Abigail and the kids gotta to
be gathered up for feeding. We all wanted to do it but Uncle
Herman says since you haven't had the pleasure before, it was to be
a special treat just for *you!*"

Eldridge's smile was pure innocence. He knew Sara trusted
him without question. He was the oldest, after all, and therefore the
wisest of the cousins.

Pointing to a chicken wire enclosure at the back of the yard,
Eldridge bulldozed smoothly ahead. "They gotta to go into that pen

over there. Need some help or do you suppose you could handle it by yourself?" He paused, looking at Sara with the same bland diplomatic grace that would later bring quiet whistles of admiration in Congress.

Roswell leaned over, poked Preston and whispered; "You guys going to church any time soon? Betcha a *nickel* they don't letcha in! *Betcha*!"

"Shhush!" Preston hissed. "Watch *this!*"

Sara, astonished at being entrusted with a real live farm chore, stopped staring at the pie plate, proudly lifted her chin and turned to seriously survey the situation. The side yard was awash with geese.

"Shouldn't be all that hard, Eldridge..." Her voice trailed off as she surveyed the problem scientifically. Properly. Gertner-like. Lofting a moistened finger into the wind, just like the heroine in Captain Mayne Reid's <u>Wild Huntress</u>, she entered into the matter of a suitably stealthy stalk.

Earlier that afternoon, to prevent the boys from badgering his gaggle, Uncle Herman had advised there were two more home place rules -- Rules of Nature regarding geese.

"One," he said with gravity, making individual eye contact with each boy. "One. Goslings scatter in a direct ratio to the speed of oncoming humans. Two. Abigail and Martin prefer to herd their progeny unassisted." Neither Rule was, of course, known to Sara. That was the beauty of it.

To the boys' satisfaction, both Rule Number One and Rule Number Two were both soon verified. Indeed, it took only six minutes of Sara's quiet stealthy circling, brisk dashes, and flat out knee-pumping runs after fleet goslings for the Van Buren's patience to wear thin. In fact, the Van Buren's had no patience at all. With a screeching banshee hiss Martin made for Sara. Wings outstretched, great head down, the looming darkness of enraged fowl pounded across crackling summer grass. Glancing up from her half-bent pose, Sara spied the winged beastie from hell and made a superb gurgling yowl in the key of A sharp which caused all the hairs on Aunt Gert's arms to spontaneously curl kinky.

Now, when one is about to die, even at a tender age, it is said that one becomes intently aware of the smallest of details. Sara noted that Martin's glistening wings appeared to be a good thirty feet across and a million tiny pointed teeth reflected sunlight in rainbows from his gaping bill.

The combination of tumultuous honking, screeches in A sharp and ominous gales of boyish laughter caused a frantic flurry of Gertner's to stream out onto the porch. They were just in time to see a beet-faced bug-eyed Sara pounding toward the low board fence separating the side yard from front lawn. The boys were struggling to maintain innocent concerned faces, but Sara's skinny wind-milling arms and legs made that impossible. Preston laughed until his eyes watered, sides ached, and he was in rather urgent need of a loo.

"Glorious!" he gasped. "Simply *glooorious!*"

About the time she cleared the top fence rail in a nearly perfect hurdler's leap, Uncle Herman glanced across to Papa Henry to opine that the girl had some speed in her when she felt like it.

"Yep," he said, heel rocking. "Pity it's a girl. Good form for a runner. Needs to keep her head up, though." A moment later,"Ouch. Now, Henry, you know that has to smart." Sara had run smack into the old crab-apple tree and loosened up a good half-bushel of little greenies.

"Ice-cubes are in the fridge, Brother Henry. I'll get the apples. No sense lettin' 'em go to waste." Studying his nephews, who were biting their tongues and minutely examining the sky, Uncle Herman shoved his big weathered hands deep into faded denim overalls, heel-rocked a moment, then strolled off to have another word with Brother George.

"George, ol boy. I think you need to spend some time behind the barn with those boys of yours. It occurs to me that Birdlegs just isn't naturally a critter-chaser, if you get my drift. Oh, and take some green crabs when you all head back. Seems we have a surplus of early windfalls."

That night back at Grandma's, out in the family woodshed, the discussion was duly held. More of a monologue actually, interspersed with "Aw, Dad! Not *that!*" and awestruck groans of "grounded for *how* many years?" Uncle George opted to spare the rod, but not the child.

Uncle Herman would have had it quite otherwise, with fervent application of a hickory switch—at the least. It seemed that not one of his radios, not even the Heathkit portable atop the breadbox, was tuned to its proper station.

Too soon, August was drawing to a close. It was time for another year's farewells and the clan's traditional picnic. Gertners piled into respective Fords, Chevy's (and one turquoise Edsel which discretely no one acknowledged) to reassemble at Uncle Herman's. This year it all went off without a hitch which nearly qualified as a

miracle but one could not say so out loud because that would surely tempt Fate. And this time, there would be no indelicate conditions brought on by Aunt Gert's special "no refrigeration needed" potato salad, a real hazard for those about to embark on three days of straight-through driving in the Chevy, what with pit-stop rules and all.

"Good thing Gert stuck to her pickled five-bean salad this
time." Uncle George whispered to Papa Henry. "At least that stuff
hasn't darned near eviscerated anyone - yet." They nodded in
solemn agreement, effortlessly recalling the frantic emergency pit
stops required an hour or so out from Hawkeyesville the previous
year. Roswell loved it.

It was getting on toward afternoon when Cousin Preston
once again felt excruciating pangs of MTBL slither up between his
shoulder blades and firmly lodge on his prefrontal lobes. Eldridge
could tell by the way his brother's eyes began to dart around and his
fingers twitch that something was up.

"No more geese-things or we'll be grounded for the rest of
our lives, 'member?" admonished Eldridge through the side of his
mouth. Preston, who somehow wasn't a true believer in matters of
eternal paternal punishment, scanned the farm for something,
anything to relieve this throbbing need for mischief.

"No geese. Yeah, I remember. No geese..." His voice trailed
off, his gaze locked on --- hydraulics.

Hydraulics. In the form of a slender silver pipe rising from
that immovable grey concrete slab over the infamous well. From the
head of the shining pipe out back, just beyond the old screened
porch, flowered a graceful curving handle. Sparkling in the sun.
Silhouetted like a wild bird's wing against a canopy of rich blue sky.
It called softly, "Prresstton, Prreessssstttonn. Here I am." Preston
was nearing nirvana.

His eyes quickly searched the crowd until she spotted her.
There she was, perched atop the fence rail, swinging those incredibly
skinny legs in the breeze. Her face was warmly pink between freckles
and glistened slightly in the sun. She looked really thirsty. That was a
good thing. That could help his cause. Then Preston recalled
something special about Cousin Birdlegs, other than she could be
dumb as a boulder about a lot of things. Ol' Birdlegs had another

key failing. Birdlegs was stubborn *and* --oh double joy -- was considerably afflicted with that seemingly infinite patience possessed by the female of the species. Yes, the pump would do quite nicely.

Sara's face lit up when handsome Cousin Preston strolled right on up to her, casually passing the pitcher. "Say, kiddo," he grinned, "would you mind getting some more water for the lemonade? Don't bother goin' in the house. There's a pump right out back there. You can get it from that." Her face lit up because she was instantly spitting mad at *dear* Cousin Preston. She knew for a fact that his MTBL affliction had had something to do with the Van Buren escapade. She didn't need to know any details. The whole mortifying mess clearly had Wisconsin Gotcha writ large all over it.

"Whadya want, Pres? More goose gettin'? Or maybe you saved back some of Aunt Gert's special tater salad from last year. And what makes you think I'm gonna leap down from here to tote your water, anyhow?"

Preston looked sheepish and kicked up a little dirt with his sneaker. "Well, Sara Jane," he confessed, "I am really totally sorry for all that. I don't know what got into me. It's a real problem. I should probably get counseling or somethin'. What do you think?" He continued to slowly swing the pitcher in a sweetly hypnotic rhythm.

"It's really hot, doncha think? Maybe you could show me how to work that ole pump and I could bring the lemonade to the folks."

Now in that day and age, toting lemonade was still a woman's job. Like it or not, it was her duty to keep the food and water fully stocked on the table. Preston wasn't about to tote anything and they both knew it. Sara's eyes narrowed and her lips began to get skinny. Then she hopped off the fence, grabbed the dangling jug out of his hand and stomped toward the pump.

"Never mind. *I'll* get it," she shot back. Preston turned away, head down, and ambled toward the picnic benches as if sorely wounded. He didn't dare look up -- or he'd bust out in triumphant laughter.

Nefarious contraptions, pumps. Especially if they haven't been used in years. It took some time for the rhythmic rusty screeching to get on everyone's nerves enough to require investigation from the grownup table. Grimly intent, Sara was unaware that Uncle Herman had come to watch. He watched for a good three minutes, noting that his niece's face looked like an overripe Better Big Boy tomato and lanky little arms trembled like warm strawberry Jell-O.

At last he reached past her, picked up a quart-sized Mason jar that had been sitting next to the pipe and poured its contents where any fool knew they had to go to get the pump to work.

"It's called 'priming the pump', honey. If it isn't primed, you can pump that handle till doomsday and never get water out of the well."

Sara looked up in astonishment and sat down on the lawn with a thump. "Till *doomsday?*" she gasped, her chest heaving from the workout.

"Doomsday." confirmed Uncle Herman.

Sara swiveled, her laser gaze aimed toward the tree-sheltered picnic tables and then fastened with undisguised loathing on Preston who was just then attempting to become one with the far side of the maple tree. Uncle Herman followed her gaze and sighed. That maple had already been struck *once* by lightning.

Now really irked, he nodded toward the barn across the road. "George, I believe it's that time again. Might I strongly suggest and recommend that a hickory switch is more effective than your citified 'grounding?' Worked pretty well on us, as I recollect."

George glanced toward his youngest progeny plastered against the tree and gave him **The Look**. [*Now, for those unfamiliar* *with this parental death ray, understand that The Look properly applied has been known to melt bones and instantaneously make all the blood in one's entire body go to dust.*]

Preston registered familiarity with this particular gaze. He was about to be dusted.

Sara hoisted herself from the lawn onto the gray coolness of the concrete slab, leaned against the pump and whispered in Preston's direction. "I'll get *you* one day, Mr. Smarty-britches..."

Summer was definitely over for the cousins, but there was one more surprise wrinkle. Homework!

To ensure that the importance of Hawkeyesville Life Lessons was appropriately grasped by her grandchildren, Grandma Gertner required a handwritten "What I Learned Last Summer" essay due back to her the first week after their return home. To cousinly dismay, this family edict was universally endorsed and firmly enforced by all respective parents. Children duly received stamped pre-addressed envelopes to Mrs. Gertner, Alder Street, Hawkeyesville, Iowa, and a "Mail By" date on the calendar circled in red. At their tender ages, they couldn't have known just how much those little letters came to mean to Grandma.

She read them fresh from the Post Office, often not waiting to arrive home, opening the first one or two to enjoy on the walk to elm-shadowed Alder Street. Neighbors would catch the sound of a bright laugh or occasionally see her dab her eyes with an embroidered hanky. Once home, her letter treasures were carefully tucked into a scrapbook of *Grandchild Mementos*" traditionally brought out again at Christmas-time to savor. Alone in the big Victorian during those increasingly long Iowa winters, but for occasional visits of Livie and Gert, Grandma found the annual letters with their sometimes hilarious, oftimes poignant Lessons Learned brought back summer warmth that lasted and lasted until long after her tea had grown cold.

What I Learned Last Summer

By Eldridge Davenport Gertner, Age 16

In olden times there were great Indian cultures in Iowa. Many of them left stone axes and stuff on the ground and lots of rivers and towns bear their names. My brother and me and Cousin Roswell (the stinky one) looked for artifacts but there were none when we got there. Uncle Herman said they were when he was young but I guess he got them all. I read Plato and Livy this summer and found out about early Roman generals and orators. I'm going to read more about Greece and Rome and the Iroquois because that's where we got our laws from. The End

What I Learned Last Summer

By Preston Dubuque Gertner, Age 14

I learned that one should never never bother hornets or bees or interrupt their lives by moving their happy home nests. They like having their houses left where they built them to begin with. Smoke makes bees sleepy but if their houses have somehow fallen to the earth you usually don't have time to make a smoky fire before they come to tell you how unhappy they are.

There are no black-striped snakes in Iowa big enough to eat goats whole unless an exotic snake has got loose from the local zoo, which they don't have near most Iowa farms. The End

What I Learned Last Summer

By Sara Jane Gertner, Age 11,
Mrs. Ellis, Home Room Teacher

The United States of America is very big. There are no oceans in Kansas or Nebraska now but there was a big inland sea a long time ago. What's left is the Mississippi River. I learned a lot of geography this summer and also about how large a goose can grow. Ganders are very good papa's to their goslings by protecting them from predators and foolish children. They make good watchdogs and make a <u>lot</u> of noise when bothered.

Our family has a big barn in Iowa made by hand because they didn't have electric tools way back then. I learned about hand pumps because they didn't have inside running water either. Boy, I learned a **lot** last summer. The End

What I Learned Last Summer

By Roswell Bettendorf Gertner, Age 7

I learned a poem from my Uncle Herman. It goes like this:

> We should not tease Our friends the bees
> Or bring the mouse Inside our house.
> God sees everything we do, And I know that this is true.
> Amen.

I remember this poem because Papa made me write it ten times and put it in my suitcase which is why I don't have the rocks and road apples I promised to bring for Show and Tell today. I also learned that we should not touch other people's things, like radios, because they aren't ours to touch. The End

CHAPTER TEN

Trixie and the Princess

"But his mother was such a *nice* little black dachshund", Mama Mattie moaned, observing the weiner dog from the litter next door had grown another four inches taller and could now easily snag stashed tidbits directly from Roswell's chair seat.

"Yes, dear, he does look a little long-leggity for a badger-chaser. And," Papa sniffed in mild distaste, "he's still pretty doggone casual about the paper training thing, too." Fastening his gaze onto Sara's embarrassed face, Papa lasered "the Look" to the hound's designated caretaker.

Sara sighed and headed for paper napkins near the kitchen sink, wrinkling her nose in near-perfect mimicry of Papa. Sensing a diversion, Roswell nudged his sneaker into the edge of the spreading puddle and began making swirly circles across the hardwood floor.

His fascinatingly artistic puddle-doodles were cut short by the fact that his faded blue sneakers were suddenly dangling a foot above the floor. The sound of slow plopping drops from his toe hitting Mama's newly paste-waxed hardwood seemed to echo in ever louder booms. Hands had a death-grip: one on Roswell's red-plaid shirt collar and the other hooked under the "Genuine and Official" black Zorro belt that kept dungarees from falling off his little backside. For a small woman, Mama had one heckuva grip.

"Touch the floor with that toe, mister," Mama hissed into a reddening ear, "and I'll be rubbing *your* nose in it!" With a dust-raising whumph, Roswell was plopped onto the back porch. An ominously shaking maternal index finger thrust right by his nose pointing toward a snake-coil of black hose at the basement stairwell.

"Wash, mister!"

Reaching back into the kitchen, Mama grabbed a frayed dish-drying towel from the bottom of the drawer and flipped it toward the offender.

"Shoes, mister. And get them clean! There will be an inspection by your *father*." Papa was *always* the threat of highest authority in their household.

"And leave the rag <u>outside!</u> Do not, repeat DO NOT put it into my wash!" Roswell was infamous for slipping nasty things into Mama's wash.

That night was a full shimmering moon and another gift was presented to the family – indeed, to the entire neighborhood. Trixie's heart was blessed by an ardent gift of song which he shared in deep throaty crescendos, mournful descants, and yodeling warbles over several octaves complete with quiveringly plaintive end note tremolos.

Early the next morning the front door's brass doorknocker was firmly rapped. It was a slow and very serious. Whap....whap... *WHAP!*

105

"It went on for 4.73 hours!" fumed Mr. Hemphill, their statistician neighbor across the street.

"No, I am sure it went on all night, dear. I am quite sure of that!" Mrs. Hemphill stood just behind her irate husband, looking a tad haggard but pertly stylish in a tailored navy-blue shirtwaist dress with brilliant white lapels. In one fist she clutched a freshly ironed white hanky with navy blue trim; in the other was an equally chic copper-red leather leash.

At the end of the leash was the wiggling incentive for Trixie's nocturnal serenades: Portland Princess of Evermont Glade. Ravishingly sweet, peachy perky and perfectly coiffed with a tiny black ribbon bow.

"Princess is in heat, isn't she?" Mama stated flatly over Papa's shoulder.

"I thought you had decided to fix things. Change your minds, did you?"

Before a retort could be made there came from the back yard, from behind the glinting four foot high chain-link fence Papa had had to erect to curtail Trixie's passion for chasing cars, a distinct yodeling howl followed by three quick yips that bounced up the musical scale. It was Trixie's signature pre-serenade intro. Earl Hemphill's face began to shade toward cherry and he opened his mouth to launch into a sleep-deprived rant. Just as he inhaled, Mrs. Hemphill passed him Princess's leash.

"Hold on, dear. Let's think about this for a moment. We may, *may* I say, have partially brought this upon ourselves."

She glared up at Earl, looked carefully at Princess, then glared again at Earl. "Weren't you scheduled to take Princess to the vet last month, dear?" Earl's mouth clamped shut. It had been crazy-making busy down at his office for over a month getting out some yahoo political appointee's crunch project. Is it possible he'd let so vital an event slip by? As vital to their peace as getting that little rat dog fixed? Personally, he was a German Shepherd kind of guy.

"Apparently the date was overlooked, dear. " Earl admitted, only because it was obvious. That admission didn't make his night without sleep any less jangling. From the back yard Trixie continued warming up for a full opus: "Baying Serenade in A minor."

Princess's warm chocolate bonbon eyes sparkled and began to melt. She was sooo in love. She began to squirm. And wiggle. She then broke into prancing dance around the porch that deftly wrapped her pretty leather leash around Maude Hemphill's legs. When it was snug, she made an elegantly athletic twist and slipped right out of the darling matching collar with sparkly rhinestones. In a flash of her "fresh from the groomer" peaches and cream colored curls, Princess darted around the corner of the Gertner's house headed for glory.

Beholding his love running to him, Trixie broke into deep bayou booming song. Princess yippity-yipped in delirious joy as she flew, bounding in great giggly leaps with all four feet off the ground. The only thing missing from the moment was a slow-motion camera and a wild-flowered meadow.

Trixie breathed deep, swelling his broad chest to focus all attention on his great five pointed star blazing whiter than snow upon a raven's back. His flat coat gleamed richly ebony. Young muscles rippled and twitched. Princess sighed. Her tail was a whirling peach-fuzz blur. She smelled of baby powder and fresh laundry. Trixie was richly redolent with whatever he'd rolled in last.

Taking the next natural step, Trixie shoved one paw into a low square of chain link and with a heavy grunt hoisted himself up. Clambering with canine determination, one foothold at a time, he went right up the fence then launched overtop with a mighty thrust of muscular back legs. It was a graceful arc that landed him with an oomph on the newly mown lawn. Shaking himself all over, Trixie began to trot in an easy lope toward his lady love. His eyes became large and sweetly luminous. His long wet tongue dangled with rakish ease out the side of his mouth. It was The Fonz bearing down on the new girl in town with debonair confidence, slicking back his pompadour with a polished flip of comb and wrist. It was Trixie, approaching his radiant goal, flipping back his gorgeous dachshund flat ears with a polished flick.

In utter joy Trixie threw back his head. Oh how he sang. How he yodeled with all that loving heart and lungs could give. Every now and then in the middle of his yearning torch song he would peek over his shoulder to note the impact of his singing. Princess alternated between cavorts in bubbly poodle-bouncy circles and adding to the din with half-harmonizing poodle ululations. Across the square patch of summer lawn they gamboled in effervescent joy, chasing tails in ever smaller circles, sprawling and rolling in passionate glee; their intent increasingly obvious.

"No, Trixie! You <u>can't</u>! Maude cried out in horror as she rounded the corner and spotted the two paw-to-paw, transfixed in each other's gaze, panting, tails a blur of wag.

"She's *AKC*!" Maude blurted. "Oh, *pul-leaze -- Don't do it, girl* !!"

As she dashed toward the pair continuing to earnestly plead, Maude's imagination held visions of peach, black, and white poodle-curly fur balls with great flat ears, long hound legs, bows in their topknots and deep voices. They were weird creatures that bayed at the moon, dug holes *everywhere* and walked with a mince. She recalled the Gertner's dismay when told that their dachshund puppy's daddy was actually a very ardent boxer.

108

Trixie made his move. "Oh merde..." was all Maude could mutter.

"Mother-of-pearl, it's no wonder that boy crooned all night." Papa and the rest of the crowd had arrived for the show.

Papa's grumpy pronouncement was followed by a quick series of semi-muttered expletives relating to the importance of neutering one's blankety-blank pets which were directed pointedly at Mama and Maude. The ladies took immediate umbrage, retorting with a low-toned spitting-fast salvo back over the net regarding the un-acted upon men folk's agreement to transport said pets to the local vet and the possible degradation of male memory with age. *That* volley was returned with equally emphatic statements relative to the timing of said vet requests and the broadcast of vitally important, yea *imperative* national baseball games, not to mention work projects.

Roswell was taking notes. He was hearing colorful metaphors never before heard at their house. Sara cocked her head. She had been staring at the strangely sincere dance of the doggies, trying to puzzle out why they were so happy and what they could possibly be so interested in that required such a dance ritual. About the time Trixie began to demonstrate proper technique for seriously pitching woo and was positioning himself for the happy nitty-gritty, Maude dove for Princess and Papa Henry scooped up the hound.

Princess could be heard yipping plaintively as her owners stalked back into their house and slammed the door. Trixie was in full throat yodel over Papa's shoulder and appeared to be nearly in pain, his eyes glazed and goggled. Papa sidled through the gate and set the dog down. He shook his head, and patted Trixie's.

"Know what you're feeling, boy. Nothing to be done for it, don't you know. Wrong side of the tracks and all. She's a real princess, boy, and you are not exactly prince charming."

Trixie stared up at Papa for a moment. Then he strode purposefully into the middle of the back yard, sat with a firm plop, shook himself into position, threw back his head and let loose with the loudest symphonic Mahler yodeling yowls to date.

Tick-tick-tick. It was the "how long can you go without sleep" clock at the Hemphill's. Papa swore that he heard an "Oh *GAD, Maude!*" rattle the Hemphill's living room window. Glancing across the street he made out the fuzzy apricot form of Princess. Pacing along the picture window-sill, she was writing love notes on the glass with a warm damp nose. Trancelike she paced, stopping occasionally to wail with plaintive poodle delicacy, staring in the direction of passion yodels emanating from behind the house just across the street.

Maternal hands in two households picked up the heavy black telephone receiver and began dialing. There was a real sense of finality in those days when you actually dialed a rotary telephone. When the clacking dial had to be rotated all the way around to the little brass bird's wing stop bar for each number, and you had to wait for the dial's humming whirl back to the start before you could begin the next entry.

"Mayfair 6-2040, Dr. Schwinn's office. How may we help you?" The respective Mrs.'s G and H tersely explained, punctuated by respective canine lovers whimpering plaintive stereophonic love calls in the background. Appointments were firmly, personally, set for the most immediate near future. This was to help ensure canine (and neighborhood) peace in their lifetimes.

Despite visits to the vet, Trixie and Princess continued to leave wet nose-skids on front window glass, pining for each other across the paved two-lane expanse of suburban Mason Avenue. Houdini Hound (Papa's name for Trixie) regularly escaped via greased lightning wiggles through the door or canine Olympic fence leaping feats, with pauses on his way to Princess's only long enough to chase another Ford or two down the street. Mama was getting pretty good at chatting up local police officers who came to the door with driver complaint reports. That didn't mean she liked it, she just did it as a mother's duty until such time as a permanent resolution to the chasing could be found. It was nearly summer and hope was warming with the sun.

Then suddenly school was out again, another grade passed -- on penalty of having to publicly explain oneself to Grandmother at the reunion! Pondering the customary process of packing clothes and prunes for four, Mama now had another crisis on her mind. Two and a half weeks at the kennel was a budget- breaker and none of the neighbors could be persuaded to take on Trixie. As a last ditch effort, she headed for the Salvatore's. Half way up the walk, she and Trixie were spotted. Living room curtains were yanked closed with a whoosh-thwack. Startled at the vehemence of a refusal before even being properly politely asked, Mama stood rooted in utter surprise. A quick series of responses – some way less than charitable – flew through her mind along with memories of having suffered through three weeks of kitty-sitting their part-Grey Smoke Persian "Poofers" who lived up to her name after every meal, often aiming fumes at Papa's pillow which was her favorite nest.

Roswell took pride in quantifying the emissions, carefully charting them by length of time and "Oh, grok!" factor. Poofers also made a non-endearing practice whilst at the Gertners of juuust missing the litter pan. This activity became lots more urgent when Roswell slipped her a hearty helping of Bush's Beans 'n Bacon before the Poofer-sized stinky-fish dinner. Back at the Salvatore's house, Trixie had decided upon his own personal response to the curtain-thwacking.

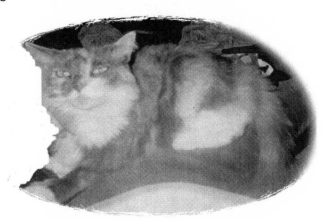

There was Poofer's flat pouty snout peaking out the window. The hound recalled how the feline not only snagged tidbits from a crockery bowl *clearly* marked "Trixie," but had for three weeks made serious inroads in his personal playtime by coyly diverting Sara.

Arching his back in an operatic bow, Trixie deftly placed an over-size-me poo dead center on the sidewalk. With a snort and quick flip of his head, he turned his back on the Salvatore's and trotted for home. Mama, who was busy being miffed, stared at swaying floral draperies, then lifted her chin, spun smartly about face and stalked away. It wasn't until half way down the block that she realized what perfect personal statement the pooch had made for her. In rapid-fire Italian, a loudly detailed description of the deed was flung after her by Mrs. Salvatore. Mama allowed herself a little smile and reached down in an unaccustomed gesture of good will to pat Trixie on the head. Trixie sighed and tugged the leash. Mama sighed and followed him up the sidewalk.

Gritting her teeth as the inevitable sank in, she walked around to the back yard gate. No way around it, there would be another passenger in the old Chevy. Trixie would have to go along. All the way to Iowa. Two and a half days. With squirming indignant "He's got his *butt* on my side, Mom" Roswell in the back seat. A distress burp popped out of Mama. She was too irked to even say "Excuse me" to no one in particular, as was her polite practice.

Later that night, after children were tucked in and Papa was humped over his study desk pondering some scientific problem for the office, Mama looked up from *Japanese Flower Arranging for Beginners* and tried to bring more clarity to the trip's logistical details.

She could not help but visualize the conflict between Papa's stoic refusal to stop the Chevy except for gasoline and Trixie's random requirement for relief. The only notice they had that "something was a-coming" was a quick heady burst of hound-peculiar scent. Mama was sure it was sulphur and brimstone. How in the name of sanity were they going to pull this off without making a stop at the Sydney Nebraska S.P.C.A.? Sigh.

Back in her pink bedroom (girl's bedrooms were *always* pink back then), Sara too sighed. "Another trek to Iowa."

An unaccustomed smile grew from a hopeful little twitch at the corner of her mouth to a full blown grin. But *this* one would be special. *Really* special. Trixie was coming! She could barely wait to show him off to cousins Preston and Eldridge who for the past two summer vacations had paraded their "Sedge" (part border collie, part mystery-date) under her nose. Trixie's presence would be defacto proof that she had at last wiggled past Mama's hard and fast pet rule: "If it's bigger than a parakeet, the answer is no!" This had for years pretty well slammed the box on pets of interest.

The day finally arrived. They were packed and on their way out of town heading toward Papa's boyhood stomping ground. It was worse than anyone had imagined.

Trixie was a happy doofus. He was going with the family on a car ride. Oh boy! There he was, tail wedged into the backseat corner, his big muzzle plopped onto Papa Henry's window-side shoulder. While this was a pretty doggone good traveling position for Trixie, it led to much mumbled prayer (at least Sara thought it was prayer) on the part of Papa whose patience gave out about the time he realized Trixie was quietly drooling into his pocket protector. While the pooch was great for short hauls, his level of fun plummeted as they sped along two-lane winding highway into the mountains, then dropped down steep inclines into the next hot valley. Trixie was not having a good time. He began burping up bits of dog biscuit into the pocket protector. Things went downhill from there.

Mama was rapidly fanning Papa with a Parade Magazine Sunday newspaper supplement while holding a hanky tightly to her nose. She was trying to keep from snickering. She knew it wasn't funny, but once in a while it was satisfying not to be the butt of Papa's jokes, but for him to get just a little of what it was like.

113

Trixie's breath wasn't nice on good days. After a thousand miles of up and down and strange climates and peculiar-tasting tap water in Trixie's bowl,   not to mention his panting mouth inches away from Papa's nose, Papa had to take action. A bright pink travel-sized Pepto Bismol bottle appeared wedged tightly between his legs. The Chevy's air blower was turned to directly blast into his face. His lips were getting really skinny and tense.

Then Trixie got sick. That's pretty much all the family remembered about the Iowa trek with Trixie. That and the fact that he wasn't allowed in the house at Grandma's and howled every night. All night. There was considerable heated discussion regarding whether Trixie would return with the family because Papa adamantly refused to have him back in the car. Grandma advised firmly that no one in the small acoustically nearly perfect town of Hawkeyesville had room or interest in Trixie. There was chat about shipping The Howler to Mr. Schroeder, Mayor of the next town and another real annoyance. Grandma sternly admonished Papa that he would just have to deal with it. Somehow they all got home.

Shortly after arriving home, Trixie chased the wrong Ford and -- as was tenderly if awkwardly explained to Sara -- they'd had to take him to a farm in the country to chase cows and he wouldn't be coming home. Ever.

Princess howled for three days. No one knew how she knew, but friends and lovers have a special sense for such things.

Earl and Maude Hemphill even said they were truly sorry that "dear Trixie" (who up till then had been 'that #$#%! pest!') wouldn't be sitting in front of their picture window barking. The suggestion that Mama might want to stop by the pound for another (preferably AKC) pooch was met with a scathing glare which she quickly morphed into a polite cough.

"I think not," murmured Mama.

Sara cried for four days. It nearly broke Papa's heart. The faint but distinctive scent of Trixie's inevitable "car ride problem" on the front seat could never be completely removed; it was a painful reminder. Papa sold the Chevy to a neighborhood kid who promptly painted it sparkling burgundy and jacked up the rear end.

"Everything has a season, Miss Sara," Papa tried to explain. "We can't know the reasons for everything that happens. We have churches and politicians for that."

Sara stared at Papa, reddened eyes large and solemn. "Then I think we're in real trouble, Papa," she whispered.

That night something with a pulsing star of light over its heart snuggled up to Sara and laid a ghostly head upon her shoulder.

"Good night, Trixie," Sara murmured falling into the dream. And there she was, skipping down a sun-burnished lane with her very best friend loping blissfully by her side.

Mamma closed her bedroom door quietly and wiped away tears that just came unbidden. She could clearly see Trixie's star beating next to her daughter's heart.

There was no mistaking that kind of love, the love that goes on past Forever...

CHAPTER ELEVEN

Bullhead Summer

The edge of eastern sky slowly turned tones of robin's egg, apricot and tea rose as the earth rolled over to face morning. Where the sun had not yet spread its warmth, the sky gave up its stars slowly, wrapped them in deep sapphire robes, and took them to the night side of the world.

It seemed Sara had barely entered Dreamland when lace curtains at the upstairs window lifted to breezes sharp with new-cut alfalfa and warming pastures. From below came smells which spoke of morning: freshly ground coffee perking into that strong brew she was not yet allowed to taste, bacon from Uncle Herman's farm sizzling in neatly laid strips within the cast-iron skillet, and the one scent that somehow always meant love and home - fresh baked bread toasting.

She pulled the quilt with its neatly stitched pink wedding rings up to her chin. This was the day she had been waiting for. After

116

considerable grumbling, Papa Henry and Uncle George had agreed
to guide her through that rite of passage rarely permitted mere girls.
"Today.." she breathed, aquiver with excitement, "I will learn how
to *fish!*"

As she tiptoed down the narrow staircase toward the source
of those tantalizing smells, carefully avoiding worn spots known to
creak, Sara caught the low laughter of Papa Henry and Uncle George
indulging in their favorite pastime, academic one-upmanship. In a
family that took great pride in higher learning, this semi-serious game
was their idea of *real* fun.

Since children were to neither be seen nor heard around
Grandma's at the crack of dawn, and especially when those elders
who were up were obviously enjoying the absence of urchins, Sara
took great care to maintain silent invisibility. In the kitchen, the topic
of the morning seemed to be literature: who could recall the most
verses and authors from those one-room schoolhouse days of
memorized lessons recited before a sniggering class of pigtail
dippers'? Uncle George was reciting:

> "A good season is summer for long journeys; quiet is the tall
> fine wood which the whistle of the wind will not stir,
> green is the plumage of the sheltering wood;
> eddies swirl in the stream: good is the warmth of the turf."

Casting a superior glance toward his younger brother, he
nodded. "Guess that one, Henry." Wagering that Henry's legendary
memory had to slip *sometime* added spice to this game.

Henry folded his hands, leaned back and seriously examined
a black speck on the ceiling. Finally, shaking his head, he sighed - a
heavy resigned sigh.

George perked up. "Great Minerva's mustache!" he thought.
"Is it possible Henry can't remember it?" Softly, he began to hum *The
Battle Hymn of the Republic.*

"Well, Georgie, it's no wonder you recall that piece. Let's see," Henry thoughtfully rubbed his unshaven chin and returned to staring at the ceiling. "Fifth grade. You sat four rows up and two seats over in that one-room schoolhouse down Goose Lake way -- when Miz Henderson was schoolmarm -- and your seat was the closest to the broken window through which extraordinarily healthy poison ivy insisted on growing."

"Hogwash!" sputtered George. "Hogwash and horsefeathers! Besides, you haven't said what it is or who wrote it. You're stalling, Henry!"

His brother smiled with afflicted innocence. "Oh, George, there was no author. Don't you remember? It's an anonymous 11th Century Irish thing. And if you hadn't broken that window with your slingshot, you wouldn't have been called on to recite the entire thing – twice." Henry's eyes twinkled. "My turn."

George sniffed, flipping bacon with a mildly theatrical air, only narrowly avoiding spattering hot grease on his lucky fishing shirt. Henry began:

> "Remember the hill; Nellie darling and the oak
> tree that grew in it's brow?
> They've built thirty stories upon that old hill
> and the oak's an old chestnut now.
> 'Member the meadows so green, dear, so
> fragrant with clover and maize?
> Into big city lots and preferred business plots
> they've cut them up since those days..."

Henry gravely bowed. "Well..?"

George lifted one bushy brow and cleared his throat. "You know I can't carry note in a bucket. Author: Will D. Cobb. And the refrain:

> "School days, school days; dear old golden rule days.

Readin' and ritin' and 'rithmatic,
taught to the tune of a hick'ry stick.."

"And a mighty stick it was, I do recall," he gravely concluded

Sara stood rooted in the kitchen doorway gaping in astonishment at the unaccustomed sound of Uncle George warbling. Papa Henry took one look at the girl, who was desperately searching for a tactful way to compliment Uncle George for the assault on her ears, and chuckled.

"Ah George, that old tomcat what courted our Miss Mercy could have done it no better!"

"Mistress Mercy," George sniffed, "apparently didn't mind, if the eternal infernal batches of kittens were any indicator of her sensibilities."

Sara blushed from tennis shoes to the roots of her snug brown braids, and fled to the front porch mortified. Reproduction, even that of pets, was a subject matter *never* to be publicly discussed in a Gertner household.

The brothers sighed in unison. "This could be a very long day..."

Despite the carefully planned loading of poles, mosquito spray, and fishing paraphernalia into Uncle George's old station wagon the night before, the sun was halfway to zenith before the Great Expedition finally hit the road. As miles clicked by on the odometer, blacktop highways narrowed to bumpy gravel road. A few clicks more and the road was tunneling through leaf-shadowed lanes bright with wild tiger lilies, yarrow, goldenrod, and Queen Anne's lace. Emerging from cool woodlands, the station wagon turned into a cow path apparently known only to occasional farm tractors or high schoolers scouting for places to neck.

For a good three more miles the crew bounced and thumped until at last Uncle George hit the brakes and the car lurched to an abrupt stop. Before them stretched a stubbled field turning to pasturage and a small stand of oak and willow casting dark flowing shadows upon a stream.

Ever competitive, Cousins Preston and Eldridge quickly cranked at respective side windows, each desiring to be the first to "smell out the fish." Relegated to the rear, Roswell sat glowering and windowless. Sara was firmly wedged in the front seat between the grownups. The youngsters detected favoritism at work here, what with only Uncle George's boys getting their very own windows. - Assured that the presence of fish could be smelled upon the wind regardless of how deep the waters where they hid, the boys thrust the entire upper portion of their bodies through the windows and pointed nose first toward the cattail pond upstream.

"Tis an ancient Indian tradition hereabouts." Uncle George intoned. "Any true Hawkeye can do it, given he has the inborn talent and proper guidance.'

The boys hunched their shoulders and took a deep *deep* breath, each wanting to be the first, just as a billowing plume of tire-churned dust passed an enveloping wing over the Ford. Survival mechanisms came immediately into play as every occupant of the Ford rifled out into the glaring sun, coughing and batting at the whirling brown cloud.

"That should be a lesson to you!" Uncle George wheezed. "A good Indian *always* waits for the dust to settle before smelling for fish!"

"Fishfeathers." Preston muttered. On this note the station wagon was unloaded, and the True Fishermen of the clan headed for the fishing hole. Sara scouted for a special place where she could practice, far away from cousins who were bound to snicker at her definite lack of expertise. Public performances were still a delicate matter.

It had been a good forty-five minutes and Sara had yet to get a nibble. She leaned against an ancient mossy skinned oak which fortunately was not inhabited by fuzzy crawling many-leggeds or winged stinging things. The girl imagined the Old Ones who once lived along the Wapsipinicon River visiting this very spot to dangle lines and commune with spirits of the place. She listened the stream gurgle as it slipped ripples around smoothed stones rising in its path. How it sparkled in those patches of light which fell between tree shadows. How deep the crystalline pools where leaf shapes echoed upon its face. The oak canopy rustled, creeper-corded branches creaking as Old Mother West wind lifted them to dust and whisper gossip from trees upwind.

The cornfield across the way swirled in long curving eddies as Mother West Wind's trailing gown flowed over golden tassels to weave a rippling tapestry. Pollen-footed honeybees sank into an embrace of silken wildflower petals. Dragonflies skimmed above the stream, their wings reflecting hues of sky. Curl-cupped leaves drifted by like emerald fairy boats. Dark twigs floated like tourists, lifting angular grey-brown fingers to point out passing sights before disappearing around the bend. A muddy Nehi bottle bobbed and rolled into a dark nest of willow roots, buried its bead and went to sleep beneath the sheltering bank. Sara imagined the leaves and twigs on a journey to the far away Gulf of Mexico and made up stories of their adventures to pass the time.

Overhead a crow looped across the sky with a darting sparrow in hot pursuit. Their aerial acrobatics were an amazement of whirling spirals. Brother Crow's annoyed hacking caw injected a strange counterpoint to the woodland opera.

Flashes of fish just below the surface taunted Sara with their disinterest in a carefully baited and bobbered line. Cradled by the oak tree, she savored scents of Iowa earth rising in waves beneath the noon sun and caught between her fingers the sweetness of honeysuckle as it wafted by. There was a coolness in that stray breeze on her arms. Eyelids drifted down to settle in reverie. Bird folk sang melodies of innocence and contentment. It was almost romantic.

But the fish were not beguiled. Shaking herself awake, Sara decided to try another spot. This was not the time to doze. After all, there was the matter of actually catching a fish!

Reluctantly, she gathered gear and moved upstream to the cattail pond where the boys expertly jiggled lines and cast x-ray vision into the depths. It was gratifying to note that they hadn't managed to tempt anything to nibble night crawlers either. Standing with feet apart just so, Sara firmly cast a long arcing line toward dead center in the small pond To the astonishment of her cousins, who hit the grass just in time to prevent impalement on the hook slicing overhead, she actually hit the water. And rather neatly at that.

Learning the art of when to dingle the red and white bobber, when to let it just drift into eddies, when the moment had arrived which required a enticing twitch - all these things she had been observing in the actions of the more learned men folk.

Pondering the niggling idea that there may not be one single hungry fish in the pond, a bored Sara let thoughts drift into the sky in search of long-tailed dragons, great mysterious faces, Moorish castles, and ships sailing among the summer clouds. it was hard to concentrate on fish on such an idyllic country day. When the pole jerked, bent in a sharp U, and taut line whizzed from the spinning reel, Uncle George shouted, "JeHOsephat! She's GOT one!"

Preston and Roswell shared a glowering glance. Eldridge grumbled, "A *girl* got the first one. Boy, if *that* isn't disgusting!" It took only a moment, however, for sour grape grimaces to pass and the boys' eyes to be riveted on the unfolding high drama. Amid shouted advice, pounding feet along the mud slick bank, and the creature's thrashing just below the surface, Sara beamed ecstatic.

Something monstrous and wonderful was about to take its place in history as Sara's First Catch. Something one could stuff and hang reverently over the mantel, something to weave memories around. Sara was so tense that she jumped when two large hands came over her narrow shoulders to grip the pole.

"That's it," Papa Henry breathed. 'That's it. Pull back, then drop the pole forward and crank like crazy. You've got yourself a big one, kiddo. A real big one!" When the point of roiling waters came close alongside the bank, Henry grasped the line with one hand, hoisted it skyward, and grinned ear to ear. Sara, who was somehow expecting it to be a fish - like a sleek trout or shining silver salmon - suddenly forgot to breathe.

Not twelve inches from her bulging eyes was a furious ebony gargoyle straight out of her worst Wizard of Oz nightmares. A huge gaping maw, big enough to swallow a tennis ball, smacked in a wetly leering grin. The massive head of the bug-eyed beast sprouted flailing blacksnake whiskers, and was followed by a good eight pounds of ugly. It was nasty. It was evil. What's more - "That is *not* a fish, Papa," she whispered through taut thin lips. Emphatically glaring at the astonished men folk she again declared, "This is NOT a fish. It's too *revolting.*" The men recoiled, aghast at such obvious ignorance.

"THIS, young lady," said Papa Henry whipping one of Roswell's notorious handkerchiefs around mean dorsal spines, "is a fat, fine bullhead catfish which you *will* have for dinner this evening. And that is that!" Mortally offended, the men folk refused to rebait her line, leaving her to mope and grope around the slimy night crawler tin in incensed silence.

Although Sara found herself unable to skewer another writhing worm onto her hook, which was just as well considering the even nastier things one was liable to catch in the pond, the day was not a complete loss. After all, the True Fishermen of the clan had managed to land a good dozen (plus one unhappy toad) before sundown and mosquito hordes called an end to their efforts.

When the triumphant providers of dinner at last rolled into the driveway, Uncle George turned to Sara.

"Missy, I think you did really well today. In fact, I think you did so well that we're not going to make you clean your catch. This is a 'you catch it, you clean it' household, but bullhead take a special knack which takes years to learn. So you can watch your Grandma this time. Next year, it's your job." Never having dealt with the barbaric business of cleaning one's catch, Sara was only mildly grateful for the unexpected compliment and reprieve.

Grandma exclaimed with delight at the fish-filled wicker basket. Humming a happy hymn, she toted it around to the back porch, followed closely by Sara who had decided she would have to watch the procedure if she were to acquire full "Fisherman" status. Settling the dripping basket on the porch, Grandma grabbed a large claw hammer, reached in with a garden-gloved hand, grasped Sara's big bullhead and proceeded to pound a great long nail through its head, firmly affixing the creature to the back porch post. With a single slash of the razor sharp paring knife she encircled the beast behind the gills, and with a practical pair of farm pliers yanked the hide right down to its tail which was deftly removed with a whack. The meat of the fish was blue. That's all Sara remembered. In later years she would recall that dinner consisted of soda crackers eaten out by the shed, upwind of frying filets.

After dinner, Roswell slipped out to Grandma's front porch and settled himself on the old wooden swing. "What a shame Sara couldn't make it to the fish feast," he snickered. Patting his bulging stomach, "Yeah, but her being gone meant more for me!" Extracting a large cotton handkerchief from his pants pocket, the same one that had seen catfish duty earlier that day, Roswell blew his nose with a satisfying honk, inspected the hanky, then stuffed it back into his pants pocket.

Roswell's hankies were notorious. Rumor had it that Mama Mattie was required to retrieve the ghastly rags with her fingertips while he slept. It was the only way Roswell could be parted from the wonderfully omnipurpose wipers of bicycle chains, hose nozzles, noses, and heaven only knew what else. Mattie, it was whispered, gravely sterilized these items before admitting them to the regular wash, and muttered strangely unladylike oaths over the boiling bleach pot.

It was also rumored that Roswell, generally quite tidy, was loathe to part with clothes made comfortable and easy from many continuous wearings. Being naturally conservative, he thought that excessive washing contributed to the premature demise of certain articles and was therefore to be avoided. If this entailed the hiding of "comfortable" clothing, then so be it. Mattie, on the other hand, was definitely of the one-wearing then-into-the-wash philosophy. It was a delicate matter of balance and compromise. And then there was the matter of the stick. That stout broom handle utilized for threats of near-term application on progeny, and for fastidiously lifting items piled in the far back corner of Roswell's closet. Again, the procedure required the boy be either away or asleep since he detested the breaking-in process of newly starched shirts and moped over excessively washed skivvies as one would over a mistreated friend. Since this was long before permanent press, the relentless cycle of cleanliness vs. comfort seemed likely to be eternal.

Early the next morning, Roswell tossed the handkerchief, now used only slightly beyond the bounds of decency, into the basement pile of the about-to-be-washed. Now it was Aunt Livie's turn to process the laundry. Dear Aunt Livie whose hyper-developed olfactory glands could at one sniff give an entire history of a child's whereabouts and doings for the previous fourteen hours.

Three steps into the laundry room, she went board-stiff in mid-stride, paled to an unnatural hue, and actually raised that cultured voice. "Henry, get yourself down here! One of those children put a *dead* thing in my wash! HENRY!"

Now when Livie used the imperative voice, even her brethren jumped to. Henry pounded down the stairs, having only heard "children," "dead," "in the wash." He didn't need to enter the laundry room to ascertain the nature of the offensive object and determine that it was not one of the children.

"Dear sister Livie," he quietly intoned, "It's merely one of Roswell's hankies. Mattie will know what to do." Livie's hand jerked up to her throat, aghast. Lifting a livid face ceiling-ward, she cast her sternest voice through the thick boards: "MATTIE! GET YOUR STICK! ROSWELL'S *HANKY* IS IN MY WASH!"

In moments, Mattie joined them at the laundry room door.

"Gott in Himmel!" she gasped as her eyes began to water. And so it came to pass that the Ceremony of the Burning Hanky became part of family lore.

As the afternoon sun slipped below the horizon, a troop of serious faced children marched in single-file solemnity toward the old fifty-gallon burn barrel. Especially for this occasion, it had been rolled far into the distant pasture behind the house, and at Livie's insistence, definitely downwind.

They marched in cadence following Cousin Eldridge to whom had fallen the part of honor. His was the suitably impressive hoe handle on which far end the fragrant cloth draped and swayed toward a martyr's end.

Bringing up the rear, toting two sloshing buckets (just in case), was the suitably dour supervisor of the deed, Roswell.

"Perfectly good handkerchief." he muttered "A perfectly good handkerchief up in smoke." He shook his head in wonder, astonished at the lengths he would go to maintain peace in the house. Papa Henry and Uncle George demurred attending due an inability to keep appropriately straight faces.

Cousin Preston, whose specialty was arson, lit off the barrel with a spectacular gout of purple flame brought on by at least two fat Sunday editions of the <u>Hawkeye Herald</u>, with supplements, stuffed one page at a time into the bowels of the barrel and thoroughly doused with purloined gasoline expertly siphoned from the Ford. The children danced around the pyre, clenched fists waving above their heads, faces gleaming in the now considerable radiant heat, chanting "Dust to dust, ashes to ashes, BURN unholy thing!" It was a thoroughly wondrously heathen display.

The Burning of the Hanky was followed in short order by the inadvertent burning of the bush, burning of the field, and near burning of the shed. Cousin Preston perched in the crab-apple tree, somehow ignoring several thousand ants, glassy-eyed in utter exultation. The rest of the clan, having been called away from the serenity of an evening's iced tea, was furiously swatting the crackling field with sodden blankets, sending up billowing clouds of sparks which twinkled like living creatures against the darkening sky.

Ah, <u>they</u> were the days to remember.

What I Learned Last Summer

By Eldridge W. Gertner, Age 17

Last summer we went fishing at a pond near the Mississippi River and caught lots. Before that we learned about aerodynamics and meteorology, which is the study of hot air, from Uncle Henry who knows a lot about it. Then we put out a big fire behind Grandmother's house that got into the medicinal garden and we all got silly from the smoke. Grandma said it was okay, it was just a pile of dead weeds for tea. It smelled like alfalfa. The End

What I Learned Last Summer

By Preston George Gertner - Age 15

One should not take gasoline from the car and burn things with it. This is morally wrong and sets a poor example for younger people. I also learned that ants bite people when you sit in their trees. The End

What I Learned Last Summer

By Sara Jane Gertner; Age 12

Fish can come in many shapes but just because they are ugly doesn't mean they are bad to eat. I feel really sorry for people who have to clean their catch because it's really nasty business. We flew kites and I was real proud of Papa because he knew all about it, even how to find lost ones. The clouds in Iowa get bigger than California and go pink on their bottoms when it's going to hail. Hail is ice from the clouds that can flatten crops and break windows if it's too big, but ours wasn't. The End

128

What I Learned Last Summer

By Roswell Richards Gertner, Age 9

You have to watch out for grownups because they'll burn your clothes if they don't like them. They will also go in your room when you aren't there to protect your own things and complain if they find messes and hit your pet rat with a broom. Parents should not have to know about pets, especially if they aren't going to be feeding it. Ralph was a good pet. He sleeped in my closet.

The End

CHAPTER TWELVE

Sow Summer

It didn't take long for Cousin Preston, acknowledged holder of the family's mechanical genius genes, to winkle open the rear window on the careening Ford wagon. Invoking the child's god of utter determination, he huddled by the balky roll down machinery in valiant struggle. The other sweltering cousins, having been crammed into the back in numbers beyond the vehicle's stated structural capacity, intoned the traditional malefactor's hymn:

"Mine eyes have seen the glory of the coming of the Ford,

We are trampling on the vintage 'cuz the grapes of wrath are bored..."

Since only melody and mumbles reached the front seat, the cousins got away with hair-raising lyrics restricted only by their prodigious imaginations.

Alternating lunging rocket thrusts with bottoming out slams onto a dirt road known as Mother Nature's Revenge, the brethren and sistren lurched toward Uncle Herman's. That they were on their way to the homestead at all, considering the radio fiasco two years earlier, was entirely due to Aunt Livie's ability to wheedle her way to success. That the visit request was accompanied by written vows of eternal goodness from the cousins (they would neither gaze upon nor touch Uncle Herman's radios ever again, Amen) only slightly shortened Herman's front porch time, rocking with the fireflies.

Cousin Eldridge, honing a talent for oration which would one day get him into Congress, was droning a nonstop filibuster into front seat ears describing individual varieties and respective expected growth rates of Mid-western field corn. Such white noise effectively covered brother Preston's attempts to replenish the rapidly depleting air supply at the rear of the wagon. The Ford's wheezing air-conditioner was proving utterly incapable of surmounting the barrier formed by three perspiring adults packed hip-wise and shoulder-locked on the front seat. Tightly closed car windows made the Ford a mobile solar collector and that didn't help *anyone's* attitude.

It was indignity enough for older cousins to be relegated to the rear-most Urchin Zone, even when heat suffocation was not an issue, but as Cousin Roswell began displaying his newfound ability to produce "silent deadlies" each time the Ford hit a rut an immediate solution became vital. To Roswell's delight, ruts were wonderfully, disgustingly frequent.

The farm was blissfully in sight when, at the very crest of the final rise in the road, Preston's mechanical efforts bore fruit. They had fresh air! Preston's eyes bulged then instantly turned russet brown as a choking cloud of Iowa dirt (sucked in via the overlooked vacuum principle) tornadoed into the station wagon. Wafting upon the roiling currents, Roswell's fragrances swiftly coiled up front seat nostrils. Retribution for Preston's short-circuiting of the rear window was temporarily stayed (he prayed for collective amnesia) as Aunt Gert laid hands upon an ample heaving bosom and gasped, "Mein Gott, what *died*?!"

Despite accusing fingers clearly identifying the culprit, Roswell's luck held. As the Ford hurtled past a battered barn-red fence, he put on his most wounded-innocent face, pointed in its direction and lied big.

"Pee-*YEW*. The pigs done it!" Grim-faced cousins agreed, opining however that not all pigs were necessarily located in the piggy-pen.

Now, for children required to exist in sanitized hygienic environments where the only tolerated scent was Ivory, such richly overpowering redolence as wafted from the pigsty both repelled and demanded closer inspection. Cousin Roswell was, of course, the first to reach the source in search of personal inspiration.

In rapid succession, arrival order generally dependent on one's length of leg, the remaining cluster of cousins gleefully descended upon the wondrous place of pigs. Despite a lanky loping gait which normally would have been used to great advantage, Sara genteelly brought up the rear. She was practicing aloof detachment this summer, brought on by having discovered a much thumbed copy of *Lives of the Saints* at the library right next to *The Nun's Story*. Being a saint seemed so utterly romantic, and their flowing old-fashioned habits, oh la!

"Adoring crowds will pilgrimage to my humble cloister just to breathe my 'odor of sanctity' Sara murmured to no one in particular, quoting a phrase from *Lives*.

"I'll carry fresh bouquets of pale lilies, even in winter, so everybody will see how holy I am. And being a saint, I can ask God to do something about Roswell - and He'd *have* to do it!" Sara sighed. It was a fantasy where she could make *anything* happen -- just from thinking it.

Setting youthful lips with imagined nunly firmness, she finished with "I gotta use the metaphysical mechanics of matter generation and lotsa prayer first, though."

Sara didn't recall the inspirational source for such a technique; it was likely born of breathing strange air under the covers whilst perusing Oxford's "M" section by flashlight.

During the endless grind of Chevying to reach Hawkeyesville, Sara sat wedged into a backseat corner with the window's roll-down knob punching into her ribs, discomfort being a saintly requirement according to *Lives*. She spent the entire trip praying for a martyr's release from such earthly woes as being too tall, too skinny, and having a mortally sinful crush on Cousin Preston. That Gertner Lutherans believed unending earthly woes were quite necessary for one's character, and had not historically been overly fond of saints, was quite beside the point. And Deacon Fleming at Sara's Presbyterian Church had positively blanched when the subject of barely teenage girls in a cloister was broached.

Distracted from her strolling contemplation by a sudden awareness of something strange in the sty, Sara stared at the rooters for a full minute and then let out with an un-nunly screech.

"What the devil happened to the piglets? They're hee-youuuu-gemous!"

Being ignorant of hog growth habits, having seen swine only in their cute stage in the *National Geographic*, Sara seized on the notion that they were observing more of Uncle Herman's legendary arcane country magic. Either that or it was a bona fide pig miracle.

Cousins Preston and Eldridge glanced furtively at each another, then grinned. Preston sidled up to Sara, now perched on the fence enraptured by the sty's residents.

"Ya know how he keeps 'em from gettin' sick?" Then he spoke more cautiously, softly...drawing closer to his younger cousin.

"It's a specially tricky trick..."

Good ol' Sara, eager for supernatural knowledge, leaned toward him and whispered back, "What is it? You can tell me. Won't tell. Cross my heart and hope to die on a fiery griddle!" The intensity of the pledge took Preston aback, but only for a moment. The deed had to be done before ambling elders reached the pig compound.

"The secret..." he breathed into her pink earlobe, becoming aware for the first time of her delicate lemon-lavender cologne and the fact that Sara was actually almost cute.

"The tricky-trick secret is -- he keeps their <u>tails curled</u> so's they don't take sick and die. If the tails uncurl for even a minute, they die a horrible death and he'll have to butcher 'em right here in front of us! For real!" Preston blinked hard for scientific emphasis, and to help him keep from busting out in howling-snickers.

Horrified, Sara swiveled around to stare at the milling hogs. "Oh, **NO**!" she gasped, hands clasped over her heart with the flamboyance of a silent film queen. Before anyone could grab a boney flying ankle Sara was up and over the fence – Saint Sara of the Sty—rapidly cranking pig's tails. To make certain they stayed tight she curled, cranked, and twisted with exceeding great vigor. This tended to irk a speckledy sow of noteworthy girth who expressed disgruntlement by performing a lightning-fast 180-degree spin.

Saint Sara was eyeball to beady eyeball with four-hundred pounds of unhappy hog.

From behind the barn, hysterical laughter from Preston and Eldridge could be heard interspersed with "Birdlegs! Oh man, that Birdlegs!" The particular tenor of triumphant cousin-cackle was unmistakable. It was their victory cry.

Sara did not hear their laughter. She was totally 100% focused on laser beams shooting out of the sow's erratically rolling eyeballs. Edging backward toward the fence, tennis shoes started sliding in suddenly really slickery muck. The sow kept on coming, encroaching into her personal space at an alarming rate of speed. Whirling in panic, Sara made for the safety of the top fence rail. Hog footwear, to her scientific consternation, provided significantly better traction than P. F. Flyer tennies.

That Sara was honestly in a real-live and for true dangerous predicament did not occur to instigators on the far side of the barn, leaning against its weather-worn sides to support a teary-eyed condition. Glimpses of wind-milling stork legs and flapping arms had been a wildly boredom-relieving spectacle.

Elders had taken the long way round from the front porch to the place where children appeared to be having entirely too much fun. Having finally grasped that the source of giggling male glee was Sara fighting to retain body parts in original non-piggyfied condition, Mama Mattie gripped the fence rail in goggle-eyed horror. Papa Henry momentarily turned away from the sight, one hand over his face muttering in exasperated embarrassment, "Oh dear God..."

It was Uncle Herman who strode into the pen, grabbed Sara's arm and flung her length in a graceful arc over the top rail onto the verdant freshly mown lawn. Turning to face the squealing milling herd, he stared steely-eyed, hands firmly on his hips. He was giving them "The Look," which worked pretty doggone well on most anything that had the capacity to be intimidated.

When they didn't respond one lick, he leaned back and bellowed, "Back off --or you're <u>BACON</u>!" The hogs stopped dead still in their tracks, stared at Uncle Herman, then placidly returned to snuffling and rooting about the sty as if nothing had happened atall, atall. The big sow plopped down in a comfy cooling mud puddle and stared right back at Uncle Herman. They had locked horns before and would likely to so again. Uncle Herman was mentally weighing out hams and hocks. The sow was eyeballing a loose slat on the fence over where it met the barn. Both were weighing viable options.

Deep into the dusky return to Hawkeyesville, thumping along in a station wagon with a rear window stuck in the down-and-open position, all cousins were remarkably silent. The possessors of two tenderized backsides, having gained firsthand knowledge of the adage "Spare the rod, spoil the child," were deep in thought. Squatting in the flat-folded backseat Urchin Zone, they were trying to avoid both the sitting position and inadvertently having a bouncing backside come into vertical alignment with another kid's face.

Roswell was curled up in a corner asleep, blissfully silent and scentless. After having been for sure identified as the source of infamously fragrant emanations, Aunt Gert had treated him to the family cure-all: 3 Tablespoons, heaping, oil of castor bean. No one had seen him after that, reading Monkey Ward catalogues in the distant outhouse as he was.

In that superior tone so dear to one's elders, Sara was asked if she had learned A Valuable Lesson at Uncle Herman's. Thoughtfully considering the events of the day, she took a deep breath and declared, "Yes. The faster one runs in pig stuff, the less forward momentum one has. I believe it's a matter of physics."

Uncle George whipped around and stared at his niece. From beneath a bushy moustache his mouth gaped in astonishment -- and undisguised pleasure.

"Why, Miss Sara, what a remarkable observation! In fact, if you don't mind, I'll pass it on to my colleagues at University." Momentarily lost in thought, he muttered "Yes, professors know a lot about running in --"

"George!" Aunt Minerva shrieked, grabbing the steering wheel, and cranking it smartly back to its proper position. The Ford narrowly avoided kissing a ditch.

Serene in her triumph, Sara nestled back into her corner of the Zone and gazed aloofly toward elder male cousins. They were glaring. And wincing. Eldridge had bitten his tongue. The Ford's careening had caused them to experience intimate contact with the solid rear door, precisely the maneuver required to renew acute awareness of certain particularly uncomfortable parts.

Sara gazed through the dust-glazed window toward a far away sky-glow that was the Pleiades. She savored this new sensation; the sweet taste of accomplishment, with perhaps the slightest hint of pride. Compliments, especially from Gertner professors, were rare treasures. It was almost enough to give a girl hope. Maybe those things of dreams *were* just within reach: real confidence and self-esteem...and maybe even an early sainthood without a stinky brother!

"Gee whiz," she thought, "St. Jude really does hear Presbyterian prayers! Wait'll Mom hears that. Bet she'll have a <u>cow</u>!"

What I Learned Last Summer

By Eldridge Gertner, Age 18

Last summer I learned about pigs I also found out that high school seniors have more productive things to do than write dumb essays like this. The End

What I Learned Last Summer

By Preston G. Gertner, Age 16

Swine have bad tempers and can kill because they are larger and faster than we think. Also, we should not put people younger than ourselves in danger, even if it was funny at the time. This is morally wrong. I know all about swine habits because Dad had me write a ten page essay on the subject I would like to use this for my biology project, Please let me know as this would be very helpful to me in class because it's already done. The End. P.S. It has footnotes.

What I Learned Last Summer

By Sara Jane Gertner, Age 13

I learned that you can't get a vocation or become a saint during summer vacation, especially if you are a Protestant. Father Sullivan said fainting during Mass at the Carmel Mission (my first!) was more likely a sign that it was hot and stuffy inside and not a sign from God that I was supposed to become a Carmelite nun even if I did faint when he was holding up the wafer. Mother Monica said you don't get vocations during vacations and that I should talk to my Pastor. I was afraid to talk to Pastor Reynolds because he'd probably kick me out of youth choir. So I asked Mama if I could be a nun. Mama said she'd have to talk to Papa. Papa said it would be okay but first I had to visit every church in town (twice!) and read a big stack of books on philosophy, theology, and myths. After going to the Episcopal, Methodist, Christian Scientist, and Presbyterian churches and reading Papa's books I talked to Mother Monica again because I had some Catholic questions. She said questioning dogma was not a good way to start having a vocation and said we should live with the cards God deals us even if they look like deuces to me.

Librarianship class starts in two weeks. I signed up. The End.

What I Learned Last Summer

By Roswell R. Gertner, Age 10

The oldfactory glands are located in the nose. This is why people smell. I would like to take kemistrey so I can know more about the oldfactory's but Papa says he doesn't think it's so good an idea quite yet. I did my required summer reading on the farm. It was called <u>The Catalogue</u> by Mr. M. Ward who is very famous. It was a story about selling things from Chicago. It was very interesting and I read it even after it got dark outside. Does this count as a book report since I am writing about it? The End

CHAPTER THIRTEEN

Orchard Summer

Summers flowed by more quickly now, and whole seasons passed between eye-blinks. The maturing cousins began to notice subtle changes in the folks at Hawkeyesville. Cousins Eldridge and Preston now towered over Aunt Livie. With head tilted back, her penetrating steel blue eyes would glare over gold half-rim spectacles as she wagged a narrow "Now you listen to me, young man" finger beneath their noses.

In Aunt Gert's chestnut hair, center parted in knife-edge sharpness, sinuous streaks of bright-whiteness made candy-striped bands in her tightly coiled chignon.

Older Gertners seemed oddly shrunken, shoulders bowed into question mark shapes, their walk more purposeful and cautious, their laughter muted and thoughtful.

Nineteen-year-old Cousin Preston had spent the day hunched amid knarly branches of a crab apple tree in the orchard behind Grandma's, distant and hidden from chore-wielding elders. In a sheltering cave of leaves, nose buried in a Russian primer, Preston was blissfully fanny-wedged between two sturdy high limbs. The battered blue thermos filled with Kool -Aid, brown paper lunch bag of oatmeal-raisin-walnut cookies, and a can of Guaranteed Kill'Em ant spray were stashed in easy reach. Everyone knew his whereabouts but opted not to disturb since the young man was actually studying.

It was a sacred task in that family of academes, studying. Crafty Cousin Roswell had been forbidden in no uncertain terms to chuck pungent windfalls up into the branches, lest the text be blessed with rotting apple mush. Uncle George, when pressed, did allow as how Preston would be fair game once down from the tree.

This taught Roswell appreciation for learning. And patience. And cunning. And guile. "It's only fair," Roswell muttered, rubbing his hands in gleeful anticipation. "Wasn't it Cousin Preston who made sure no one else would perch in the orchard when he wanted to be there? Wasn't it Preston who got the perching idea off Sara just yesterday, and put her off perching by dabbing blackberry jam under the bark of her favorite nesting branch?"

Roswell recalled it had only taken a few minutes for his sister to cascade out of the crabapple, shirt and Bermuda shorts loaded with swarming berry happy ants. Forbidden use of the only bathroom in the Victorian, lest the creatures decide to make it a new home, Sara had endured the indignity of standing "stark nekid" in a corner of the dank cellar as a rusty stream splattered down from the ancient Sears showerhead. There was no shower curtain.

The pipes were supposed to channel solar heated rain run-off from the attic collection tank, a progressive and practical idea in the early 1920s. But the previous night had been a mite nippy and the hot water tank's pipes long since rust clogged. This resulted in her having to endure not only "full Monty" cellar exposure to whomever wanted to wander down stairs, but tepid brown streams dribbling over her goose-bumps. She didn't know what she had done to offend God, but it sure seemed like He was making her sit in the Celestial Humble Seat a lot.

She had snuck a glance into the dark overhead rafters, "I'll bet there are more creepy spiders up there than that two-holer out by the shed." She shuddered and tried not to ponder nasty slithery things lurking under the wood-slats nekid feet were standing on. She scrubbed a little faster with a sliver of brown Ivory soap pried from an oxidized green soap dish.

"Awfuller and awfuller," she muttered.

Now the view from that particular corner consisted of either a wall of concrete blocks crumbling away before one's very eyes (revealing huge river rocks in their middles), or long pine board and cinder block shelves of cobweb-draped jars. She could just see the pints of preserves of quince, crab apple, elderberry, mint-berry jelly, and those infamous jars of ten-year-old rhubarb which had to be fatal by now. Sara dared not think overlong about the bottom shelf with its lamentably long line of lima's marching into the shadows.

Out of curiosity, she stared beyond the open shelves, just making out the strange jumble beyond. The cousins were not allowed free roam of the cellar, being confined to movement to the washing machine from the clothes chute basket. There was just too much trouble and temptation beyond those boundaries.

In the dim light she could see chairs hanging bat-like, feet up, from overhead rafters. Two long-barreled .22 rifles dangled by dry leather straps next to three nasty-rusty rabbit-traps. A carved bedstead rested its richly dark finish against tangled piles of machinery later identified as a disassembled printing press. No one could remember for sure why it was there. Aunt Livie recalled something about a deal for temporary storage back in 1949 when the Hawkeye Herald upgraded to fancy new machines. Then Mr. Meuller died and no one seemed to know or care it was there.

None of this mysterious history could be pondered for long, though, lest one forget the distinct possibility of spiders silently descending into one's hair in search of blackberry-smeared ants. Sara refocused on getting clean, dry and clothes on!

Later that same night, Preston snickered from his upper bunk. He chuckled for several minutes, then off-handedly informed Eldridge tucked in below.

"She may have gotten a coupla inches taller since last year, but you could still play xylophone on her ribs..."

Eldridge's eyeballs popped. He whipped straight up in bed promptly beaning himself against the upper slats. (The boys had long since outgrown the stacked red twin beds but there was no where else to bunk at Grandma's so whatcha gonna do?)

"You *pre*-vert! You watched!" he hissed.

Preston laid back, tucked hands under his head, and grinned wide.

"Yeah... and she's got chest bumps, too..."

Burying his head under a lumpety pillow smelling of age and mothballs, his brother groaned.

"You're gonna die early, Preston. Fer really sure."

Smirking toward the ceiling, Preston decided it had

been worth hiding behind that bee-infested bush just to sneak a peak through grimy cellar windows. It was even worth painful jabs of Aunt Livie's cane and then having to make up a lame story about searching for Roswell's lost softball. (Aunt Livie thought there was definitely something wrong with a boy who spent ten whole minutes with his head stuck into a bush).

"Wowzah yowzah, she's gettin' to be a looker," he mused from the upper bunk, "but still a bit too scrawny for my refined tastes."

Eldridge groaned again. He was more interested in local political campaigns and chess than girls, but even he could recognize signs of impending disaster.

The next morning, Roswell stared up at Cousin Preston perched in the crab apple tree and pondered. Letting the unthrown windfall drop to the grass with a sodden thump, he ambled toward Grandma's kitchen. He was trying to justify a plan of action that just screamed to be set into motion. He thought of the time Sara hadn't ratted on him about the green snake between her sheets, and the time she had smuggled him an albino laboratory mouse following Ralph the Rat's untimely demise.

He finally concluded that it was time to do something distastefully unnatural for him -- a thoughtful Good Deed for Sara. It would be a first. Roswell's world pretty much revolved around Roswell; doing for others generally meant doing for Roswell first.

This one's for the Gipper," he said with grim determination. As the well-soaked "Guaranteed Kill'Em" label slurped off the can, he reasoned, "It's time for a Hero to enter the scene, and it might as well be me!"

Roswell had had no practice whatsoever in the Hero business, but thought it might be time to begin. The new need to be seen in a positive light had been strongly motivated by Mama's disquieting observation that not only was her son blind to his own pettiness and self-centered nature, but had increasingly seemed sympathetic to the" plight of poor misunderstood bad guys." Not a good sign, she opined, passing him booklets entitled: "Right and Wrong: How to Tell the Difference" and "Saint Francis of Assisi: Lessons For Children."

Roswell patted the back porch. 'C'mon, Sis, sit down here next to me. Want you to see somethin' real special." Caution born of considerable past experience made her hesitate, but that chubby face radiated cherubic innocence.

"Oh, all right. What is it - more snakes? Dead crickets?!!"

"Naw....," wounded righteousness trembling in his voice. "Just sit and watch. Pulleeze...?" Roswell had long since mastered the art of appearing innocent, even when caught smack in the middle of the dastardly act.

The kid was right. It was well worth watching. Shortly Roswell and Sara were treated to a satisfying spectacle as bug-eyed Preston rocketed out of the crab apple tree, pounded pell mell through the orchard, over the bank and belly-flopped into Muddy Crik. Ten minutes later, he stomped back toward the house putrid reeking from matted head to squishy tennies. Squirming muddy ant balls, amidst other vaguely recognizable tidbits, clung and hung on his dripping clothes.

It seemed that in addition to transferring the Kill'Em label to a can of stuff guaranteed to enrage Mr. Ant, Roswell the Avenger had chunked bushel-baskets full of composted garden waste and fresh cow pies into the creek. Iowa mosquitoes had done the rest.

Sara stood and slowly stretched. Tucking hands into snug blue jean pockets, she turned and stared down at Roswell in shrewd admiration. With a hint of twinkle in her eyes, she spoke. "I do believe this cancels out the snake, Roswell. I do believe it does."

"But not the crickets'?" whined the boy, taken aback and suddenly alert.

"But not the dead crickets you put in my milk. They were tied to fishing weights, remember?"

"Oh Yeah..." Roswell gravely recalled the deed. "You get me for that next year, okay? I don't think Aunt Livie can take any more from us this summer."

Sara glanced in the direction of the orchard. "Next time, Brother Roswell, it's my turn." She ambled back to help with dinner -- making certain for all their sakes that rhubarb was not on the menu. Roswell sighed and with surprising perception murmured, "Birdlegs had better get a tutor. She isn't mean enough to come up with anything really good on her own. Better yet, she needs a full time Hero."

Dinner proceded uneventfully. No rhubarb, no birdseed, no parakeet pie. After the china had once more been tended to and tucked away, Sara headed out to the sidewalk for her customary post-dinner walkabout..

As she looked at the family orchards, and let her gaze wander over the fence to corn rows marching in the setting sun, she began involuntarily practicing her "remembering" exercises. Catching herself, she realized that she might really not be able to remember such peaceful beauty when she got really old, like 35 or so. These memories might be crowded so far back into her brain that they would fade clean away. Oh, horrors!

Bounding back up to the porch, she dashed inside, sprinting upstairs to her room two steps at a time. Ricocheting up the stairwell behind her was the unmistakable and stern Raised Voice With Clipped Syllables...

"Sara Jane Gertner, proper young ladies don't gallop through the house like wild horses. Especially not in this one! Do you *hear me, girl!?*"

After five anxious minutes rummaging through her blue Samsonite suitcase, she emerged triumphantly with a spiral-bound notepad with just enough pale green pages to journal "scientific birds-eye observations". Descending the stairs with as much calm grace as she could muster, Sara then had to convince Mama and the aunts that it was absolutely necessary (and safe) for her to hang out in Hawkeyesville Park for a couple hours.

"Well, it *is* only eight blocks away," Aunt Livie observed. "With St. Margaret's on the east and our Lutheran church on the west, it should be quite safe." Aunt Livie believed that no one in their right mind would be so rash as to sin in front of *two* churches.

Aunt Gert weighed in with the practicalities. "And, my dears, it's plenty close enough for Henry or George – or even one of us for that matter – to happen to drive by without seeming too nosy." The aunties nodded.

"Bingo!" thought Sara as victory approached. "Let's hear it for Aunt Gert and her practical "can do's".

"Well, Sara. I guess it would be ok. But you need to be back before it gets too dark. Do you need a dime for the phone? Do you need a map." Sara shuddered.

"No thanks, Mama. I have a coupla quarters," fishing them out to make it obvious that emergency pocket change was close at hand. The alternative was toting an odiously obvious ladies hanky with coins knotted into a corner "just in case you need a ride home." It was embarrassing overkill for an eight block hike. It was what you made a kid do, a public sign that parents didn't believe you could think your way out of a dill pickle-jar.

And then she was free, blessed with an extra dime from Aunt Livie (just in case), she marched double-time down the porch steps toward liberty. On the sidewalk Sara paused, mentally flipping a nickel to choose which direction to head. To her right was Alder Street stretching toward Route 61, across the railroad tracks and into town. The way was shaded by thickly leafed oaks and elms, bordered by Victorian, Craftsman, and new ranch style red brick houses. The walk past neatly mown lawns and tidy geranium beds. This was the most familiar route. This was the *safe* path.

To her left, an unpaved street lead past a low white-painted cinder block honey processing plant. Surrounded by beehives, red clover and a full artists palette of wild-flowers, it emanated a particularly delicate aroma when bees were at their busiest. Sara could almost taste the freshly harvested comb honey Mr. Goodstein dropped by every week. He was very sweet, and so was his honey. Sara recalled many a wonderful ramble down Honey House Lane.

As daylight faded, the lane began to shade into colors of dusky honey which flowed past the plant in a single-lane ribbon. It continued over the rise by the water tower following Mother Nature's natural contours then dipped out of sight toward the farmer's bridge over Muddy Crik. Branching off Honey Lane was a footpath which, after much scenic meandering, eventually led back to within a couple blocks of Hawkeyesville Park. Although its most frequent users were rabbits and foxes, it was an enjoyable alternative for strollers and joggers.

Sara glanced at the sky and that pretty much made the decision for her. While Honey House Lane was an amusingly diverting meander during early morning hours, it was already late afternoon and would soon be dark. Who knew what lurked beyond that rise in the road, just out of sight? Sara shuddered. Rabid rabbits? Black garden snakes? Hidden gardens?

"Lima beans. Probably big patches of nothing but gooshy wild lima beans and if I got lost in the dark that's all there'd be to eat. Only thing worser is liver, or maybe succotash." Suddenly Honey Lane did not feel like the "safe path" for her journey.

Now, straight ahead was the corner where Alder Street met 6th Avenue. It was, depending on who you talked to, where Alder either began or ended. On one side of 6th were corn-fields and wildflowers, on the other tidy two-storied 19th century homes. This was, after all, the edge of town. And this was, it appeared, the zen "middle path" offering a modest taste of excitement and a moderate bit of safety.

Early glimmerings of dusk settled along the eastern horizon; Mother Nature was already pinking the dawn on the far side of her empire as Sara set out.

Across Alder and up 6th Avenue she went. On the porches she passed, she could sense alert small-town curiosity from folks rocking slowly on their front porches. There were curious stares through thick spectacles. Sara could almost hear their thoughts.

"Bless Pat! Now, why on earth do you think that girl should be in such an all-fired hurry on a humid August afternoon? She likely has no sense, and she's certainly walking way too fast for this heat. Whose is she anyway? She doesn't look like she's from around here, oh it's Missy *Birdlegs*..."

As she strode out of sight, the porch people returned to their unhurried rocking with an aloofness born of practice, whispering to the wind that young people these days just had no good sense atall.

And there was the park! God, how she loved this place where trees great-grandmother old shadowed a place for once delightfully empty of people, and delightfully peopled with grey squirrel, blue jays, and rosy-breasted robins. At the edge of the park were bronze water fountains, spring fed and all natural. She paused, relishing their burbling coolness, savoring its mineral-rich bite as it filled her mouth.

Thus readied for a long spell of diligent work, she picked an auspiciously situated table, dusted the faded red bench seat, and plumped herself down. Sara had had her choice of picnic tables, it being mid-week, coming on dark and all.

For a while, she just sat there watching, filling her senses, as evening winds ruffled high boughs of elm and hickory and oak. How to begin, what to say that would entice the memory of an old person of thirty-five, how to properly revisit and reveal this day to a future mind --a mind which most assuredly would be cluttered with serious grown-up stuff.

Her attention wandered. Seemingly of itself, her pen began to catch brief thoughts, moving, flowing effortlessly along the pale green lines. The Iowa sky deepened past robin's egg into sapphire, shading to mystical indigo around flame-edged clouds. Atop ornate iron poles beside winding park pathways, the electric lights flickered on gleaming brilliant-white and grey-silvered-green, sending leaf shadows up into dark swaying branches.

"The long ago meander along the Pennsylvania Turnpike through Allegheny mountains enrobed in shawls of pale mist. Hearing someone croon 'Allegheny Moon' on the radio and remembering to remember the scene..."

Words flowed on as day grew old and faded away.

Sara sat back in amazement. Hadn't she just *started* writing? How had the spiral notebook pages filled up like that? Why was the ballpoint pen skipping, half-forming random letters as its ink supply failed? So intently focused on her world of thoughts and observations, Sara had been oblivious to passersby who glanced inquisitively in her direction. She had been oblivious to Papa and Uncle George who drove by slowly, making certain she really was at the park, and was okay. Uncle George shook his head in quiet admiration.

"She has an amazing ability to shut out the world, Henry. May it stand her in good stead." It was the closest thing to a blessing that Papa had ever heard from his brother. Then he looked at his daughter with different eyes, appraising her as she *could* be years from now. The possibilities were certainly there. It made him glow with pride. "She'll make a fine professor one day," he tenderly agreed. It was the closest he could come to a genuine approval rating.

"Just a little bit more," Sara was talking to the ballpoint pen. "Just another coupla lines. I want to remember all these buildings, the smell of the creamery, the bronze mailbox dials at Mrs. K's Post Office..."

Biting her lip in total concentration, Sara hunched back over the picnic table. Forearms pressing into the scarred planks became embossed with initials of lovers, bored kids and Time. Tucking straying tendrils behind her ears she absentmindedly flicked at annoying gnats looking to cruise up her nose. Sara wrote until daylight and ink were both quite exhausted, and her hand had cramped into a claw.

Finally, she reached the point where she couldn't find one more margin or tiny space in which to write. She closed the spiral notebook, automatically printing date and subject on the upper right corner of the cover. She had made the effort. She had done her best. Sara just hoped that these carefully captured memories could be reclaimed in that far distant future time, that this little notebook wouldn't be accidentally tossed or lost as she navigated the linear line of life. She was startled when she realized that it was really dark, that the sky was awash in Milky Way stars and Orion had hunted his way well toward a midnight rendezvous. She felt for her quarters and the spare dime for the phone.

"No." she firmly decided. She stood up straight, shoulders-back, and then did a couple ballet-yoga stretches. She was a big girl now, and could walk eight doggone blocks without supervision or Aunty rescue. So there! She picked up the notebook, carefully threaded the pen into the spiral, hooking it firmly then headed for the Victorian at 6th and Alder retracing her original route.

As she walked, she stared up at the neat procession of old fashioned cast-iron streetlights. Through their spotlights danced a chorus line of gnats, velvet-winged moths, and lumbering Iowa mosquitoes. Dark swift shapes zipped through the footlights of the "6th Avenue Show," darting into existence from farm fields black as nothingness. Squeaking brown bats wheeled and darted, skimming edges of radiant halos like gulls above ocean surf, feasting with delicious abandon.

Now, folks back at the Victorian weren't the least bit worried about Sara strolling home alone down either Alder Street or 6th Avenue. Hawkeyesville was a close-knit family town, after all, and AT&T had not yet forced the removal of Mrs. Hansen, their town central telephone operator who could locate anyone, anywhere, anytime. Grandma merely cranked up the old wooden wall phone and requested her school-chum Ethel Schroeder-Hansen to ask if anyone would mind keeping an eye on her granddaughter. Pleased to oblige, Mrs. Hansen had then rung up Widow Meyerson whose living room window bordered in banks of pink violets provided a perfect vantage point to watch Sara at the picnic table. Widow Meyerson kept vigil over her charge, rocking and crocheting yet another bright-hued afghan for the Lutheran Church Ember Days Bazaar. When Sara departed, Millie Meyerson just rang up Grandma with a terse, "She's headed back in your direction, dear."

This was the way they had kept track of each others progeny for decades; ever since the first community telephones (and Mrs. Hansen) were installed. Local youngsters all agreed that discovering the great secret of the Watchers Network explained the curious phenomenon of parents knowing gory details of escapades they had participated in way across town. It also explained why parents would be found waiting on the porch, slowly whacking a freshly cut hickory switch against the railing, when offspring ambled back up the walk.

As Sara sauntered along, the gentle eyes of Watchers kept pace with her progress from one corner to the next. In a sense, she later considered, this particular progress was bittersweet. For the more elderly Watchers, it might well have been the last time they saw the skinny-legged girl they'd watched grow up summer by summer. After the following year, the summer of her seventeenth birthday, it would be fifteen long years before she returned to stroll the quiet haunts of Hawkeyesville. By then, Mrs. Hansen's Watcher's Network would be merely local legend; few would recollect Sara had been their dear "Birdlegs" who worried about getting warts for lack of grace.

Sara continued her walk, but with an unnaturally bright twinkle of amusement in her hazel eyes. Smack dab in the midst of her journaling "Life in Hawkeyesville," Sara had been inspired along a completely different vein. It was all about balance, she decided. All about "what goes around comes around." It was all about – A Plan. Very careful execution was required so that no obvious meanness could be detected. This prevented beatings --and the possibility of public performance disaster. Sara had it all worked out down to the tiniest, finest detail.

"Tomorrow," she breathed in keen anticipation, "Tomorrow there's gonna be a primo numero uno 'gotcha', dear *dear* Cousins, and it isn't gonna be another Birdleg's roast either." Her quiet cackle of impending triumph sounded wicked. It was gonna be wicked wicked good! She just *knew* it.

CHAPTER FOURTEEN

Birdleg's Revenge

Since early morn Cousins Preston and Eldridge had been out in the back pasture, east of the crab-apple orchard, whacking away at an entire year's wealth of burdock, biting nettles, and wild sun-gilt hay with the two-handled scythe. At least Preston was whacking. Eldridge, eye-balling the wicked long blade and noting a high probability for self-inflicted damage, wisely chose to observe. Equally certain that nasty rodents were lurking in the tall grass just waiting for a taste of toe, or worse, he held forth perched on the top fence rail.

"Don't stop now, Pres! We gotta get this done before the folks get back at three o'clock, or there'll be no county fair for us!"

With powerful grace, the scythe continued rhythmic slicing arcs through the dry underbrush. Preston stopped, breathing heavily from the hard work of scything, and swept a sun-browned forearm across his face to reroute sweat dripping into his eyes. He leaned on

154

the scythe's curving handle, then suddenly grimaced as every shoulder muscle took the opportunity to simultaneously cramp into Boy Scout knots.

Rubbing his shoulder, Preston hollered from mid-field toward his lounging brother.

"So, how about dropping your butt off that fence and pitching in before I keel over flat!"

"Or are you still afraid that 'things' might getcha out here in the grass?"

"It's not my fault..." Eldridge shouted back, banging dents into the railing with his heels. "If Uncle Herman hadn't told us about those nutzo farm rats, why I'd be right down there with you. Yessir, I sure would!"

"Right! You bet! " Preston muttered, then retorted with a zinger.

"Know what? You're just a -- a *slacker*!" Preston grinned. It was the worst epithet in the family vocabulary.

Eldridge gasped, then angrily chucked the scythe honing stone he'd been juggling toward mid-field. He was aiming for kneecaps.

Quickly eyeballing the incoming projectile, Preston merely reached out, plucked it neatly out of the rushing air and stashed it in the sweat-damp pocket of his khaki shorts.

155

"I didn't letter in softball for nothin', ya know! And what's this '<u>we</u> gotta get this done,' lazybones'? You got a *rat* in your pocket?"

Preston knew he was pressing his luck, but just couldn't resist.

"Ya know," he brashly continued, "I hear rats can sneak right up a fencepost, get into a guy's britches when he's not payin' attention, bite him on the hoo-hah's and *he'd-never-know-they-were- there-till-it-was-too-late, Eldridge.*" He was exasperated.

Eldridge's face turned the color of cherry vanilla ice-cream. He was angry, alarmed, and a little nauseous all at the same time.

Well, it *was* all their Uncle's fault. Ten summers ago, they had been mesmerized by good old Uncle Herman's creepy bedtime tale of an avenging hoard of farm rodents who crept upon a sleeping farmer and "did him in good" for setting out traps instead of sharing from the bulging corn crib. At the time, Preston had thought the rodents properly justified, the old farmer having had corn to spare, after all, and Brother Rat having a family to feed. But Eldridge, who had just managed to slam into puberty with a vengeance and had a heightened sense of protectiveness for bodily parts, promptly developed a full blown phobia based solely on the midnight tale's tragic ending. It didn't help when Cousin Roswell, inspired by the tale's retelling, had acquired snaggle-toothed Ralph the Rat for a pet.

Preston returned to thwacking neat semi-circles with grim determination. "I'm gonna have to do this all by myself," he muttered.

"But," he brightened, "that means *I alone* will get the glory - *and* the trip to the fair! Well, well, well. Maybe things are lookin' up around here!"

The sun neared a caldron-hot zenith over the field. Eldridge had been sitting on the fence rail so long there was a groove across his backside. Supervising could be thankless work!

He complained, "Hey Pres, I'm starving. It's bloody scorching out here, and I' m getting – ugh!- *sticky!*" He plucked at a limp cotton shirt in distaste.

"Well, ya know everybody's out at Uncle Herman's 'cept us," Preston glowered, "but remember -- Cousin Sara said she'd whip up something real memorable for lunch. That sounds pretty promising, eh? And Aunt Mattie says she's cooking pretty well these days, as long as you don't want biscuits or gravy or lima beans cause she doesn't do those."

"So if you're so doggone worn out from perchin' up there..." he pursed his lips and looked superior, "Guess *I'll* have to stop working and go clean up. Why don't you head for the house, Eldridge. Stick your head in the kitchen and lemme know what's cookin', okay?"

Shoving hands deep into corduroy pants pockets (carefully, lest something furry had crawled in there), Eldridge sauntered toward the kitchen, muttering, "Yeah, and your socks smell like a dead horse, Preston. Not that you'd notice since you're sweatin' like a horse and all..." Manual labor was so distasteful.

Laid with a crisp white lace tablecloth and second-best china, the dining room table sparkled in August sunbeams streaming through the tall dining room windows. There was enough silver and glassware clustered around each plate to serve at least three extra diners. Sara had come to love dramatics, and such over the top touches of elegance. Besides, she'd planned carefully for this gotcha and it had to be done up right!

Waiting until the boys were properly seated at table, hair wet-slicked back and suitably attired in clean shirts (and socks), she made her entrance, gracefully sweeping through the swinging kitchen door bearing a fragrantly steaming china platter. Then she went back for the covered bowls, returning to place them with a gracious flourish before the ravenous boys.

157

Eldridge reached for the nearest lid, not even waiting for the Gertner grace "Thank you Father for this food" to be intoned. He was promptly rewarded with a smart smack across the knuckles.

"Not yet", Sara demurred. "Patience is a virtue, Cousin. Be virtuous."

"...and make us truly grateful, Oh Lord, for all that we are about to receive," the boys prayed, heads bowed, eyes flicking with anticipation from one covered dish to another.

"Amen" the three chorused. At last it was time.

"Now," Sara inclined her head toward the bowls, "You may serve yourselves. And let nothing go to waste!" Wastefulness was a biggie sin at the Gertner house, considered an offense of the first water.

"Say hey, you don't have to worry about that!" Eldridge chortled, lunging for the biggest platter. As he lifted the lid and revealed the main course in all its glory, his face paled and jaw dropped. He set the cover carefully upon the tablecloth.

"Sweet Jude," thought Eldridge, stunned speechless. "She can't be serious. This can't be happening."

Reaching across the table with both hands, he snatched covers from every bowl, then sat back with an audible whompf. Ominous gurgles were coming from somewhere under the table.

Preston, too, was staring. He stared past sparkling glasses, taking in the steaming bowls one by one. Two stomachs now gurgled in foreboding unison.

Sara cast her most innocent "Who me?" Roswell glance around the table. "And may you be truly thankful."

Rushing on before the boys could recover their wits, "And you have to eat every little bite cause that's all there is in the fridge. I worked very hard, slaving over a hot stove *in this weather* to make this especially for you. So don't you be making me feel badly."

Glancing toward a Eldridge who was paling past vanilla ice cream well into cauliflower, she continued, "Besides, I understand from your mother that this is your very most favorite dish."

How Sara kept a diplomatically emotionless face without bolting kitchen-ward in gales of giggles would never be known. The boys were contemplating a bolt for the kitchen, too, but were undecided as to the timing: Now, or after they'd tried to consume what had been so 'lovingly' served?

Artfully arranged on the main platter were great slabs of liver: charcoaled crispy black on one edge, real close to raw on the other; a condition which took masterful maneuvering of the cast iron skillet to achieve. Sara had also avoided seasoning – neither onions nor bacon nor old jalapeno's would disguise these innards!

Lurking along the bottom of a large bowl patterned in Old Roses were rigorously overcooked leftover lima beans garnished with a fistful of gone-to-seed parsley and one wilted rosebud.

Beside the butter plates, in the boy's very own personal cereal bowls, quivered lime Jell-O with black things inside and a loathsome lemon sauce drooled overall. This was her most creative culinary adventure. Sara had steamed old raisins and stuck cloves into each and every one. To the casual viewer, the plump California raisins now had a most lifelike creepy-crawly appearance, like water bugs trapped in quivering green sap.

"We ran out of milk, so I fixed cherry Kool-Aid to accompany our feast. I think the colors most complementary, don't you? A little green, some pink..?"

She took great pains not to make eye contact with her cousins nor to gaze overlong at the table herself.

"Go ahead, dig in! I nibbled while it was cooking so I'm not really hungry anymore." The boys could quite understand that.

"But there are *big* steamed black prunes stuffed with peanut butter and icing for dessert so be sure to leave room!"

To their extreme credit, the cousins played the part of gentlemen. They emptied bowls and platters down to the last dripping morsel. After politely excusing themselves to "return to labor in the fields," both bolted at an extraordinary rate for Little Muddy Crik where they encamped in humid heat for the next hour apparently loosing their prunes.

"No more scything today, my, my..." Sara whistled as pots and china slipped beneath foaming Ivory suds.

"Isn't that just too bad. Guess the boys won't be going Scott County Fair after all since the field isn't finished..."

Opening the round-top fridge, she lifted Mrs. Wimpel's best-effort-County-Fair-recipe chocolate cake from the bottom shelf, settling it with care on the kitchen sideboard. Then out came fresh cold cuts from the Main Street Meat locker, three kinds of creamery cheese, and a half-loaf of Grandma's freshly baked wheat bread. A whopping fat kosher dill nested on top. Sara hummed a sparkly tune of satisfaction.

"Plen-ty of sunshine, co-ming my way. Zippity dooo dah, zippity aaay, My oh my, what a gloooorious day ..."

Cutting an overly generous slice of cake to go with lunch, Sara paraded into the dining room. Through the tall windows, she could just make out hairpin forms of two guys being "definitely indisposed" in the bushes by Muddy Crik.

Turning back to the table, Sara seated herself, folded hands and reverently bowed her head.

"Dear Lord, forgive me for having wasted food and for telling a couple big fat whoppers, but since I'm gonna get a licking when the folks find out anyway, You don't have to worry about it. Okay? Thanks. Very Truly Yours, (and I really mean that) Sara. Ahhh-men."

Hazel eyes twinkled. The smile was pure Mona Lisa.

"Super supreme numero uno *hot-gotcha!*"

CHAPTER FIFTEEN

And Then…

"Ohmigod, that's a *great* picture, Sara. Isn't that the one Dad took? And look at you -- complete with the famous world-class-ugly hat. Whatever happened to that thing? Did it wash up with the kelp

after Roswell chucked it overboard?" Sara responded with a deep hearty chuckle. Preston handed back the dog-eared souvenir amazed that she had hung onto it, but then Sara was a legendary packrat of memorabilia.

The family fishing trip on Monterey Bay had been a big success for the two in the picture who landed seventy-eight pounds of rock cod, ling cod and a couple flounder which came up flat and heavy as an iron bathtub. Nearly everyone else was lima bean green, sprawled on the deck or draped over the bow rail.

"No idea what happened to the old chapeau, Pres." She shared. "Guess it's kinda like socks that vanish in the washer; ugly hats and socks have a way of going walkabout into another dimension."

The pair were reminiscing, passing time as they made their way from the Lutheran Church to the old Victorian on the southernmost edge of town.

Bang! Bang! Wham!

Preston stopped dead in his tracks and whipped around to see where that sharp battering sound had come from -- and to make darn certain-sure it wasn't one of *his* kids. Sara laughed in sympathy. She was doing a lot more laughing these days, more than she recalled doing as a kid in Hawkeyesville.

Bang! Whappity-BANG! The racket was insistent, loud and impishly familiar. "Look at me" it said. "Listen to me" it proclaimed in brash boyish echoes.

Sara grinned, mischievously nodding toward the front porch of a harvest gold and moss green Victorian. On a new front porch swing sat a twelve year old boy, dragging toes of his Nike sneakers on the freshly painted floor, thwacking the shuddering old trellis on his mighty backswings. Nothing had changed.

It was kind of the new owners to let them visit the old Gertner house, but a shocker to see so much changed although – the porch swing thwacked into the trellis again – some things hadn't really changed at all. Preston grinned. The grin faltered as he actually *looked* at the yard. The cousins had been responsible and accountable for carefully, regularly, mowing, edging, weeding and trimming the hedge exactly plumb-level straight. Now a flock of pink plastic flamingos grazed randomly amidst the crabgrass. Gnomes with red-painted hats and plaster bunny rabbits peeked out from beneath hasta and blue hydrangea bushes.

"Steel yourself, Pres. They painted her room purple. There are plastic beads hanging across the doorway and "KISS" rocker posters thumb-tacked to the wall."

There was a hissing intake of breath from a thunderstruck Preston. "In the 'sanctum sanctorum'?! And Grandma Gertner hasn't shown up to haunt them?" He shook his head in utter disbelief. It felt absolutely sacrilegious. He winced as the trellis took another thumping hit. For a moment he felt like he'd been thumped as hard as the trellis.

As children, even as young adults, the cousins had rarely been allowed to even so much as peek through the doorway, much less hang out in Grandma's personal space.. They remembered feeling awed respect when first allowed to gaze upon her six foot carved headboard and heard stories about all the babies (aunties and uncles) born on it, far out in Iowa territory. It was a first-class-fine bed. They remembered dark green window shades, pastel print wallpaper and long lace curtains. Cousin Eldridge had the bed now, along with hand-crank wooden telephones which he used for home intercoms, and he had the old back porch wooden ice-box, too. Or was it Preston who inherited the ice box? Sara couldn't remember all the details of the estate disbursal.

"They're mostly all gone now, you know." Preston shared. Sara nodded. She'd been on the road for years, working as a project manager all around the country and Europe. She hadn't had nearly enough personal time to visit with the elderly aunties and uncles before they passed on. There was a certain guilt about that, the feeling that she should have somehow *made* time, come up with a scientific linear time-stretcher or something.

Eldridge had passed the Wisconsin bar with flying colors, and had developed a reputation as a true-blue scholar. His skills in management, oration and fine Gertner-style teaching made the Aunties proud; Uncle George and Aunt Minerva certainly were. It seemed miraculous but of course one couldn't say so because that would surely tempt Fate. Although Eldridge developed a finely wry sense of humor, he never cottoned up snuggly close to his children's pet rat – a present from Roswell, naturally.

Preston had done his time teaching at University, slogging his way through political crises, managing to drag the administration kicking and screaming to happiness in the 21st century. That, too, was considered miraculous but, on the other hand, quite expected of a genuine Gertner. His reward was being tapped to head an international economic advisory group. Not entirely sure that that was just reward for all his pain and effort, he did allow as how the pay was a heckuva lot better. Everyone had kids.

No one knew what really happened to Roswell, and frankly at the last no one really cared to know. He was a lost soul who had determined as a grown up that right, wrong, and truth were whatever he said they were at any given moment and were completely fluid concepts. He was also in permanent denial. Sara occasionally lit a candle for him; she knew that God would get in the last paddling and hug, and that karma would balance everything out.

"So, Birdlegs, did you ever figure out the difference between girls and boys." It was an old joke between Preston and Sara.

"Oh-my-yes," she blithely exclaimed. "It has now been *scientifically* proven that boys were all wired backwards at the Factory. In fact, EPA and OSHA shut it down for retrofitting; they have six months to revise their business processes, get Level Five certification, and bring it up to meet the more stringent standards required for the female operating model."

Bang! Whappity-BANG! The trellis shuddered. Preston burst out in an uproarious belly laugh. Sara knew for a fact that if he'd had a mouthful of milk, she'd have gotten him to Full Spew, maybe even Nose Spew. That, too, was an old joke.

She took his hand, patted it a couple times and then became very quiet. Sara looked deep into his jet-lag bone-tired eyes, leaned over and kissed his cheek.

"Thanks, Pres. Thanks for all those years, and all those memories. And thanks for coming all the way from Zurich. I knew you'd want to be here for this."

"You worked hard to make this happen, Sara. We all thought about it, but you were the one to take action, and you of all people had the least amount of bandwidth. Kudos, gal, kudos from all of us."

Preston checked his watch. They needed to get back to the park. A small crowd had gathered around a freshly dedicated bronze bust of a strong featured woman. She was clear of gaze, firm of purpose, with a sweetly wry smile. Her head was crowned by a thick coiled braid, the way she had looked until very late in life. Affixed to the rose granite pillar was a gleaming bronze plaque:

"AURELIA SCHROEDER GERTNER MEMORIAL PARK,
HAWKEYESVILLE, IOWA.
COURAGEOUS COMMUNITY LEADER,
WISE COUNSELOR, LOVING MOTHER. "

In smaller print was the phrase insisted upon by Sara and seconded by the remaining cousins. They smiled softly, reminiscing. Hearing with memory's voice their darling Grandma Gertner.

"CIVILIZED PERSONS DON'T COMPLAIN.
THEY MAINTAIN DIGNITY AND BY GOTT
FIX THE PROBLEM."

And Sara had finally fixed *her* biggest problem. Now in her mid-30's, she had the most beautiful legs in the history of the world - - at least that's what her adoring husband told her. And even if he was pulling them just a little bit, and even if they were still plenty bowlegged, well that was fine with Birdlegs.

She had finally found that "Happily Ever After" hoped and prayed for every Hawkeyesville summer, without fail – for years.

Additional Acknowledgements

To Cliff, for bringing Grammy Birdlegs her "Happily Ever After"

dreamed during summers in Hawkeyesville.

ABOUT THE AUTHOR

Lynne Johnston Lewis has been crafting humorous fiction, poetry, historical research, technical articles, and other literary works for decades. Recipient of five national awards for technical and fictional articles, she is a published poet, national conference speaker, I.T. project manager/road warrior, and certified Consulting Fellow Asset Manager. Additionally, she's an accomplished photographer, artist, landscape gardener, historic home restorer, backyard archaeologist, amateur electrician, and breast cancer survivor. Listed in *Who's Who of Women Executives 1991*, and *Who's Who of American Women 1991-92*, she has several works of photography and fiction in progress.